HELL'S GATE

Edward M. Grant

Banchixi Media
Canada

First Edition, 2014

Paperback
ISBN-13: 978-1-927549-24-7

eBook
ISBN-13: 978-1-927549-25-4

Published by Banchixi Media, **www.banchixi.com**

CHAPTER ONE

June 14th, 1852

The house loomed over the cliffs like a castle protecting a land so desolate and remote that no sane man would want to be king. A cart rattled along the cliff-top path, and the horses' hooves thumped on the dirt as it rolled to a stop. Hope sat in the back, on the piles of luggage and supplies, and turned her head for a better view.

The grey walls of the house, topped by battlements and towers, rose against the dark storm clouds. Atlantic waves smashed against the rocks far below, filling the air with the salty smell of ocean spray, and screeches of seagulls wrestling for fish. Iron spikes topped the tall black stone wall around the estate, and rusty metal gates sealed the only gap, locked with a padlock and chain. On the far side, an up-ended cart kept them shut.

William, her father, pulled his horse to a stop beside them. He had bought the stallion in the village, claiming there wasn't enough room in the cart after they filled it with whatever food and supplies the villagers were willing to sell them. More likely, he just wanted to pretend he was back in the cavalry. He would have looked every inch the cavalry officer if he was wearing his uniform, and he had always sounded much happier in his war stories than Hope ever saw him in his business life.

Her brother, Henry, sat on the saddle in front of him, and twisted around to see the view. "Are we there?"

The stallion snorted as William stared toward the building beyond the walls. "This is how they described the house. But it does not look welcoming to visitors."

Hope smirked. "Has Uncle Howard ever been welcoming to visitors?"

Perhaps he would even turn them away. An early return to London from this damp wasteland would be worth another week of boats, carriages and trains.

The rear of the cart rattled. Pat, the village farmhand her father had hired to drive them and look after the horses, stood there, smiling at her while his dark eyes studied her face. She could hardly even guess his age, as his skin was tanned from working outdoors, and the wrinkles on his forehead could have come from years or sun. Or both.

She stared at her Bible, pretending she was engrossed in Leviticus, but God's warning against unnatural relations with relatives and animals was more distracting than Pat's smile.

William lowered Henry to the ground, before dismounting himself. Eliza, Hope's mother, sat on the bench seat at the front of the cart beside Mrs Phillips, the housekeeper. William took Eliza's hand as he helped her down.

"Ay, miss," Pat said.

She looked up. Pat held out his hand toward her. She put down the Bible and took his hand, but looked at the ground, not his face, as he helped her down.

"All right, miss?" he said.

"Thank you, I am fine." She turned to look toward the house. Her legs ached from sitting cramped in the cart, and her stomach was glad to be back on solid ground after hours of bumping along the track.

Pat helped Mrs Phillips from her seat. William rattled the chain, but the padlock held it firmly in place. Metal letters spelled out a word in the rusty ironwork of the gate. Hope reached up, and ran her fingers over them.

"Tartarus."

Greek for Hell. Was that Howard's idea of a joke? Or did the name bring him there?

"They say that Saint Patrick once found an entrance to Hell in Ireland," William said. "I hope Howard was not so unlucky."

Pat joined them. "Hello, miss. And sir."

"Perhaps there is another way in. We could follow the wall and search for it."

"Perhaps we should just leave," Hope said. "He is clearly not expecting any visitors. Or desiring them."

Pat stuffed his cap into his pocket, and the gates rattled as he grabbed them. "I'll climb over, sir. Maybe I'll find something."

William nodded, then cupped a hand around his pipe to block the wind as he lit it. "I really do not want to return to that village tonight. See what you can do."

Pat pulled himself up onto the gate, and put his foot onto the bar that ran across the centre. Then he took hold of the spikes at the top of the gate and pulled himself higher. He lifted one foot, to swing it between the spikes at the top. He grunted as he pulled himself up.

Then his hand slid from the spike, and he fell back.

Hope gasped. Pat stopped his fall, pulled himself up, then turned his head and smiled at her. "Fooled you, miss."

William glared at him. "Pat, the ladies are tired, and we do not have time to waste on tomfoolery."

Pat swung a leg over the gate, then swung the other. The wooden cart on the far side creaked as he climbed down onto it. He swung his legs over the side of the cart, then, with a loud crack and a grunt, he disappeared behind it.

Hope stepped forward and took hold of the bars. "Are you all right?"

"This wood is rotten, miss. Broke when I grabbed it."

"I am going to look for animals," Henry said. "There must be lots living around here."

"Henry," William said. "Stay close."

Henry ignored the advice and ran out onto the moors. He found a bush and shook it, then found a hole in the ground, broke a branch from the bush and prodded the hole with it.

Hope kept an eye on him as he explored, but would rather be looking at the view out to sea. The land they had passed through along the cliff tops in the cart was barren and rocky, with stunted trees so twisted and bent that they grew almost horizontally.

William walked to the edge of the cliff, and puffed on his pipe as he gazed at the ocean.

"Why are the trees like that?" Hope said.

"The Atlantic wind deforms them."

She could understand why. She pulled her shawl around her as the gusty wind shook the branches and blew the heat from her body. Surely the trees would feel no more comfortable there. If only Herbert was with her, to keep her warm.

William pointed out to sea with his pipe. "If you were to jump down and start swimming, the next place you would find yourself would be America. There is nothing between us to block the wind at all."

Hope looked where he pointed. Water stretched westward to the dark clouds on the horizon, interrupted only by the white foam where waves broke out to sea. If she swam, she would be very tired by the time she arrived on the other side.

"Revelations 9:2," William said.

"And there arose a smoke out of the pit," Hope recited from memory, "as the smoke of a great furnace, and there came out of the smoke locusts upon the earth."

He nodded. "Not bad. Keep studying."

Every few moments on their journey, he had called out a chapter and verse of the Bible and expected her to recite it. She had studied as diligently as he demanded throughout the trip, by train from London to Liverpool, over the sea to Dublin, then canal and coach across Ireland. Even though her mother crossed herself every time she saw a Bible, for reasons that seemed to make no more sense than anything else she had done since she last saw Uncle Howard.

But did her father really know every verse he requested? She hadn't been brave enough to make something up and see whether he nodded when he heard it.

The cart on the far side of the gates shook, then rolled away. Wood scraped against the metal bars as it slid down, then away from the wall, making room for the gates to open. But they still had to find their way past the padlock.

William strolled back to the gate, the wind blowing his pipe smoke into Hope's face as he puffed on it.

"Can you see any other way in? Or a way to open the lock?"

Pat's face peered back at them between the bars. "The wall goes as far as I can see, sir. Down to the cliffs one way, and up behind the house the other."

"Perhaps you could find a ladder," Hope said.

"Perhaps, miss. If I spent the rest of the night looking."

"Howard should be there," William said. "Walk to the house and get him to open the gate for us. We have wasted enough time already."

Pat nodded. He put his cap back on and strode over the rough grass toward the house. Now the gate was clear, they had a better view. Howard's house was a stark contrast to the small cottages thatched with straw in the nearby village. It was much taller than it was wide, and topped with a solid slate roof between the towers.

The lifeless, stone eyes of gargoyles stared down from the wall beneath the battlements. Hope could see little detail from that distance, but they had wings and horns, gaping mouths full of very large teeth, and widely spread legs which revealed that they were definitely male.

The whole estate would have seemed more at home in a foreign land, almost as though Howard had brought it there himself when he returned from overseas. That would have made more sense then believing he had found it there.

Pat stopped outside the house, studied the large wooden doors at the top of a set of dark stone steps, then crept up to them with his cap in his hands. He knocked on the doors and waited, then strode down the steps and walked around the side.

"Perhaps Howard is not here," Hope said.

"Knowing him, you could be right. He is the kind of man who would ask us to visit, then leave on some childish quest."

Moments later, Pat reappeared on the far side of the house. He strode back.

"No sign of life, sir."

"We must get through these gates somehow."

Pat glanced up at the sky, which was darkening above them. "The house is locked too, sir. Perhaps we should return to the village before the weather gets worse."

William looked behind them. Mrs Phillips sat, knitting, on a weathered rock beside the cart, and Eliza sat silently beside her. Eliza hadn't spoken since they left the village, and said little enough while they were there. Her father had said the fresh air would improve her health, but all the travel seemed to have worsened her mood. At least it seemed to have improved his.

"It would take all night," William said, "and I will not make the ladies travel another twenty miles in that thing. Howard did invite us here, and will understand if we have to find our own way in to the house. Besides, if he was sick enough to ask us to come to his aid, he could be unable to come to the door."

Pat grabbed the broken cart on his side of the wall.

"Perhaps if we moved both carts by the wall, you could all climb over without too much strain."

"The ladies will not be climbing, and that rotten cart would not support them anyway. I will join you, and together we will find a better way."

"If you say so, sir. I still reckon we should head back to Graiguengal before it's too late. I'm sure you could find rooms at the inn until the old man comes back. It's not like they're busy this time of year."

William tapped the tobacco from his pipe and slipped it into his pocket, then put his hands on the gate and his foot on the bar. He pulled himself up.

"I will come too, Father," Hope said. Her dress was hardly designed for climbing, but she was tired of reading the Bible, and knitting seemed no more enticing.

Henry whacked the bars with his stick. "Me too."

William swung his leg over the gate and frowned at them. "You will stay there. Both of you."

"I can help them over," Pat said.

William climbed down the far side of the gate. "No. My daughter will learn to behave like a lady, and my son does not have the constitution of an explorer."

Hope gazed through the gate at them. "Father, I do not want to be left here wondering what is going on."

"Entertain your brother and mother while we search for a way into the house. They will need something to do."

"Father..."

"You will not question my decisions any longer. Wait here until we return."

He turned away, and strode toward the house.

Pat watched him for a moment, then walked to the gate and held up his arms. "Come on, miss," he whispered. "I'll help you."

"And me?" Henry said.

Pat smiled at him and winked. Henry grabbed the bars and began to climb. Hope studied the gate. Her arms weren't strong, and her legs couldn't stretch to the bars in her dress. She pulled a case toward the gate from the cart, then stood on it to reach the first bar, before pulling herself toward the top. Pat helped Henry down the other side.

"Look away, Pat," she said, then hiked up her dress as she swung a leg above the spikes. She sat between them on top of the gate and lifted her other leg, but her heel caught in the dress. She twisted her foot as she tried to pull it free, and her hand slipped on the wet metal. The dress caught on a spike and tore as she slid back. She opened her mouth to yell.

Pat grabbed her. "Lucky I didn't look away, miss, or I'd be picking you up off the ground."

He supported her as she pulled the dress from the spike. On the other side of the gate, Eliza glared at her, and Mrs Phillips lowered her eyes, pretending to concentrate on her knitting. Then she was free, and Pat helped her down. His hands held her hips longer than he needed to, his strong fingers pressing against her skin through the cloth.

Henry was already running toward William as her feet touched the ground.

"Father, Father," he yelled.

Hope pulled away from Pat before William turned at the sound of Henry's shouts. He stopped and waited for Henry to catch up, while Pat and Hope strolled to meet them.

William watched their approach. "What did I tell you?"

"I am old enough to make my own choices, Father."

"I would just send you back over the gate, if that would not make matters worse." He glared at Pat. "Do not encourage my daughter in her ambitions. Of any kind."

Hope turned her hips, so the torn edge of her skirt flicked behind her, where it would be hidden from him.

"Father, Pat did nothing, except help me down when I was already over the gate. And we are here now, so let us be useful."

William opened his mouth to speak, then shook his head and turned away.

The wooden doors of the house were large and solid, but battered and scratched as though something had tried to break through them. Two cross slits had been cut through the wood, recently from the look of the light brown wood against the weathered grey of the rest of the door. A solid padlock on a thick chain through the handles held them shut.

"Father, look at this," Henry said.

On the wood, someone had smeared words in brown letters. *Go Home.*

CHAPTER TWO

"Do you think someone wanted Howard to leave?" Hope said. Had the locals decided that mad Uncle Howard was no longer welcome amongst them? That might explain why he barricaded the gates.

William huffed. "Knowing Howard, I'm sure everyone wanted him to leave. But he would certainly not have taken their advice. If he is not here, it is because he chose to leave for his own reasons."

He climbed the steps to the doors, set within a solid-looking porch. On the ground floor, thick metal bars covered the glass of the windows, and those at the front of the house were too high above the ground to see the interior. A few panes were smashed, and wood showed behind several of them.

"Perhaps they came here and tried to throw him out," Hope said. "That would explain the locks and broken windows. And why they did not want us to come."

"They did not seem unhappy enough to do that when I spoke to them in the village. But perhaps they were trying to hide their crimes."

What did he mean? The raven-haired girl in the village had told her that, when one of the local girls vanished some time ago, the villagers came down ready to lynch Howard as a devil-worshipper, before he saw them off with a rifle.

"Do you think they killed him?"

Pat put his hand on her arm. "Miss, the people around here don't much like strangers, but they're no murderers. If anyone attacked a place like this, it would be smugglers looking for a place to hide, and I haven't heard of them around here in years."

"Indeed," William said. "Let us not jump to conclusions. First we must enter the house, then open the gates before your mother decides to make her own way back to London on foot."

He lit his pipe again, then walked down the steps and along the wall of the house. Henry ran down the steps behind him and followed. Hope followed them at a more leisurely pace, and Pat accompanied her.

He looked up at the gargoyles. "Funny-looking place this, miss. I've heard tales, but never been here."

"My uncle had just returned from his service overseas, and wanted to get away from people. I could hardly imagine a house that suited him better."

"Sounds like a funny old man."

She smiled. "That he was."

She looked up at the front of the house, then at the view of the cliffs and ocean from the doorstep. Howard must have sat inside, happy in his seclusion for the first time in years. No-one in their right mind would come there to pester him, and, if he bought supplies from the village every few months, he would otherwise have no need of human interaction.

William studied the small windows in the base of the walls. More metal bars ran across them to protect the glass. Hope crouched beside one, as well as her dress would allow, to peer in. They provided light for the cellar, though not enough to see the interior through the window. She pulled on one of the rusty bars, but it was solidly fixed into the wall and wouldn't move an inch. They wouldn't enter that way.

At the side of the house, another door opened onto the lawn. The ground rose high enough to peer into the windows beside it. Planks of wood covered them on the inside, and more bars on the outside. William rattled the door handle and pressed against the door, which wouldn't move an inch.

He banged on it. "Howard?"

No-one responded.

"I'm bored," Henry said. "I want to explore."

"Do not go too far," Hope said. "We don't want to lose you, too."

He ignored her, and wandered off across the lawn.

She followed him, while William continued his stroll around the house. The sky dimmed as black clouds moved in from the ocean, and, from the look of them, the weather would soon be both cold and wet. They would have to find shelter before the storm reached them, if they didn't want to freeze overnight.

Henry ran into the yard, and Hope followed. Coal was piled high in a lean-to behind the house. Enough to last Howard for months, probably though the entire winter.

"I reckon there's something that will keep you warm, miss."

Hope glanced over her shoulder. Pat smiled at her and strolled past, toward the moss-encrusted well in the middle of the yard. Opposite the house were the stables, of brick and faded wood. Several planks were broken or missing, and others hung loose.

The stable door swung open in the wind, tapping against the frame. Hope approached it, and something moved inside, then tapped against the door. It swung back, and she stepped toward Pat as a shape appeared in the shadows inside. Then the door swung wide open, and a deer ran out. It bounded across the lawn, toward the wood of stunted trees that grew beyond the gardens.

Pat smiled at her, and she realized she had grabbed his arm in her surprise.

"Nothing to be afraid of while I'm with you, miss."

She released his arm. Couldn't the man find something else to do? Still, his presence was reassuring in case they did find some wild animal more dangerous than a deer. She strolled to the stable, and Pat followed. They peered into the darkness. No horses were inside, nor any sign that any had been stabled there recently, aside from the worn saddles and bridles hanging from the walls.

Henry shouted. They hurried to the door and looked around the end of the stable. He stood on the lawn with a big smile on his face, holding a large metal keyring with a dozen or more keys.

"Father," Hope shouted.

He appeared around the far corner of the house and strode toward them.

"What is it?"

Henry held the keys above his head and jangled them.

"We seem to have found Howard's keys," Hope said.

William took the keyring and examined them, then dropped them in his pocket.

"Where did you find them?"

Henry pointed toward a spot on the grass, between the well and the wood. William wandered over to it, studying the grass as he walked, then crouched to examine the ground.

"Howard," he yelled.

Henry joined in, loud enough to be heard in America. Hope walked toward the wood, shouting as she went. If Howard was sick or injured, perhaps he could hear them and call back.

Rain splattered on her dress. Just a few spots at first, but the dark clouds above showed that worse was to come.

William handed the keyring to Pat.

"Unlock the gate and bring in the cart."

Hope, William and Henry waited at the steps, under the cover of the porch, as the rain grew heavier. Pat drove the cart to the house with Eliza and Mrs Phillips on board, parasols protecting them from the worst of the drizzle. He stopped at the foot of the steps and climbed out. His hair was slick with rain, and his wet shirt stuck to his skin.

"Keys, Pat," William said.

Pat threw him the keyring. William unlocked the padlock and pulled it from the chain, which rattled through the handles as it fell to the ground. Pat stood close beside Hope, and moved even closer as William unlocked the doors.

His warm breath blew against her neck. The heat of his body warmed her back.

His rough hand grabbed her ass.

Hope stepped away and fanned herself with cold air as the blood flowed to her face and her cheeks glowed. Had the others seen anything? No, they were too preoccupied by the clicking of the keys as her father unlocked the door.

Pat leaned forward, until his lips were beside her ear. Could he hear her heart thumping?

"Sorry, miss," he said. "I thought you might feel faint after all that travel and walking. What with all this excitement I might have to catch you if you fell."

William pushed the doors and they opened slightly, then stopped. He pushed again, but they opened no further.

"Let me help, sir," Pat said.

His hand brushed against her ass again as he passed her, then he glanced back and winked. She scowled. Herbert would have shown him the error of his ways, if her father had allowed him to accompany them. Her father would too, but then they would be without help for the rest of their stay.

Pat ambled up the steps. His arm muscles flexed beneath the wet cloth as he pushed the doors, then he slammed his shoulder into one. It rattled, but held firm.

He slammed against the doors again, and wood cracked. Hope crept up the steps to see inside as Pat and William pushed again. The doors finally opened.

Wooden boards inside the house had been blocking their way. They clattered to the floor as the doors opened into the darkness beyond.

CHAPTER THREE

Hope knew Uncle Howard was reclusive, but to lock himself inside a house and board up the doors? What would drive a man to such extremes?

"Father, do you think Howard's illness had progressed to the point where he decided to keep all visitors at bay?"

William stepped into the doorway and stared into the dim interior. "No matter. We have come this far, and I will not turn around without finding him. If the sickness has claimed him, we can at least give him a Christian burial."

Had this spot ever seen the light of God's love? For all she knew, and from the look of the surroundings, it might have been part of Satan's domains since the beginning of time.

William looked back at the cart. "Eliza, wait on the porch. It will keep you dry."

Eliza didn't respond, but Mrs Phillips seemed glad of the words as she sat huddled beneath her parasol on the cart. She smiled and nodded at William, then helped Eliza off the seat and led her toward the steps.

William and Pat stepped through the doorway, while Henry played with the chain and padlock on the steps. Hope followed them inside, any fear of catching Howard's disease overcome by desire to see the kind of house her peculiar uncle would choose to live in.

The entrance hall would have been dark at the best of times, but, with no candles or gas and the windows boarded up, she could see only shadows in the dim light from the door.

"Pat, fetch a lantern from the cart," William said.

"Where do you think Uncle Howard would be?" Hope said. "These doors do not seem to have been used recently."

"Howard?" William shouted. The word echoed around the house, the echoes rising upward through the staircase at the end of the hall.

Hope heard a faint mumbling. Was that Howard's response? As she listened more carefully, she could only hear scratching. A house of that size in a desolate part of the world, particularly if left empty, would inevitably become a home for rats.

"Howard?" William shouted again.

They waited for a response, until Pat returned to them with the lantern, illuminating the corridor with its faint glow.

William pushed open the first door, on the left side of the hallway. They looked through, into the dining room. Boards were nailed over the inside of the windows.

They stepped inside. The table was bare, other than a thin layer of dust glistening in the light from the lantern. No-one had eaten there for some time.

"Let us bring some light in here," William said as he walked toward the windows.

Pat handed the lantern to Hope. The scratching was more frequent and closer, and she shone the light into the corners in case rats had found a home there. If they were near the kitchen, the animals would have a ready food supply.

William and Pat pulled on one of the boards. After a few heaves it came free, and the fading daylight illuminated the room near the window.

Hope crept past them, keeping the lantern light low where rats might be. Dust coated the skirting boards, and small paws had left prints among it.

Growling came from the far corner. Her heart jumped, and she held out her arm as she swung the lantern toward whatever might be hiding in the darkness.

She backed toward the windows, moving to the apparent safety of the daylight shining through them. William and Pat crept toward the noise. With the window behind her, she could at least see whatever it was, if it decided to attack.

William picked up a rusty poker as he passed the fireplace, and lifted it to shoulder level, ready to strike whatever he found. The metal lantern hung heavy in Hope's hand, and would do as a weapon if she had no better choice.

The low growls came from the door in the corner of the room. Had some animal broken into the house and attacked Uncle Howard when he was too sick to protect himself? She had never heard of dangerous animals in Britain. How could a man-eating creature find its way into a house in Ireland?

Or could Howard have brought one back with him? A bear, a lion, or a tiger, perhaps? Or something worse.

William and Pat reached the door, William still holding the poker ready to strike. He nodded to Pat, who reached for the handle and turned it, then pushed the door open and stepped back.

Nothing rushed out, other than a rotten meat smell which filled the room the moment the door opened. Hope covered her nose with her handkerchief, but the smell still found its way through. Her stomach churned again.

William peered through the doorway, then motioned to Hope. "Give me the lantern."

Her heart thudded as she crept around the table toward the door, stepping lightly to avoid making noise, and listening for any creatures who might have made the dining room their own hunting ground. The growling seemed more distant, as though the creature had backed away on seeing the door open.

She handed the lantern to William, and he motioned for her to back away. She took two steps back. The smell was worse, but, having made the effort to approach the danger, she had to discover what it might be.

They looked through the doorway. A thin, scraggly black dog sat on the steps, glaring at them. William lifted his foot to take a step toward it, but Pat moved first. It backed away.

"Hello, boy," Pat said. "What are you doing here?"

He took a slow step toward the dog, and rubbed its head. It stopped growling, but continued to watch them.

"Howard?" William called.

Could the dog have been guarding Uncle Howard in his diseased state? Perhaps he was lying downstairs, awaiting their rescue?

William crouched and examined the dog. He lifted a metal tag from the collar, and moved the lantern closer to read it. The dog looked back at them, his tongue hanging out as he sat back on his haunches.

"Hello, Kerberos," William said.

Guardian of Hell. He could only be Howard's.

Pat waited at the top of the steps with the dog as William descended them, and Hope followed close behind. The lantern illuminated the open cupboards, pots and table of the kitchen. The contents of the cupboards were spread around floor, and much had been chewed. Howard must have left Kerberos in the kitchen, and Kerberos had done his best with the resources he found available to him.

It also smelled like a sewer. Rotted and salt meat were scattered across the table and floor, and the food and water had worked its way through the dog, who had then done what came naturally.

"Pat," William said, "there's a lot of clearing up to do before Mrs Phillips can work in here. We will search the rest of the house before the ladies come in."

Pat nodded and descended the steps, and Kerberos followed. William and Hope climbed back to the dining room, and into the hallway. Further along it, the door on the right was locked, and William tried the keys on the keyring, one after the other.

On the third try, it clicked open.

Behind the door was Howard's study. Books were scattered across the floor in front of an armchair, some open to pages in languages Hope couldn't understand, others closed, but book-marked. Blankets were spread over the chair, as though he had used it for his bed.

Jars containing red and green liquids stood on the bureau against one wall. Whatever was inside was so thick that it barely flowed as Hope picked up a jar and turned it around in her hands. She twisted open the lid, held it to her nose, and sniffed. The vapour almost burned her, and she quickly sealed it again. Could Howard have been attempting to cure his sickness with remedies he learned abroad?

The greatest peculiarity was a collection of a dozen or more clocks. Most were stopped, and the others showed different times. How much of his day had Howard put into winding the clocks to keep them all running? Why did he care so much about knowing the time?

In one corner of the room was a gun cabinet, with several shotguns and muskets leaning against a rack. William lifted a musket and placed the butt against his shoulder.

"Good old Brown Bess," he said. "Howard must remember his army days."

He placed it back in the rack, and lifted out one of a pair of pistols, weighing it in his hand. He turned the cylinder at the rear and read the writing stamped across it.

"Colt Navy revolvers from America. I have yet to see one, but Howard already has two. I must be in the wrong business, my dear."

A tall bookcase stood in another corner, the shelves packed full of books, behind thick, glass-panelled doors. By the door was a collection of walking sticks and umbrellas in an elephant's foot, one topped by a silver gargoyle which resembled those that adorned the house. Had Howard based the stick on the house or the house on the stick? Either way, the rubberized raincoats hanging from hooks showed that he had come well prepared for the weather.

The outer door was locked. Metal hoops attached to the wall allowed a wooden bar to hold it closed, but the bar leaned against the wall by the elephant's foot. Perhaps Howard left that way and locked the door behind him? To have barricaded the house against any intruder, locked himself out, then lost the keys in the garden would seem an ironic fate.

Along the corridor were more rooms full of furniture covered in cloths, that they could use as a lounge and living room, and below the stairs was a large locked door. William tried every key on the keyring, but none would fit the lock.

"This must be important," William said. "The lock is unlike any key on the keyring."

"What could be behind it?"

"I suspect it leads to the cellar. There is no space for a large room behind it, and little enough for stairs."

They banged hard on the door and called for Howard, but received no response.

"Should we call Pat?" Hope said. "Between us, perhaps we could break it down."

William put the keys away. "No. If Howard was there he could not fail to hear me. If he returns, I do not want to have to explain the damage to him if we broke in."

"Are you really sure he will return?"

"For your mother's sake, we must assume he will."

William looked up the stairs. Even if Howard was in the cellar, near to death from his illness, there was nothing they could do to save him, short of carrying him back to the village, and then on to a doctor.

They continued their search upstairs. The house contained many bedrooms on half a dozen levels, and, on the topmost floor, steps to an attic. Crates contained clothes, paintings and other souvenirs of Howard's travels. A door in the roof opened out onto the battlements, and they strolled around the narrow path, looking at the gardens below.

The altitude gave a good view of the surroundings, but no more sign of Howard than from lower down. No bedrooms showed any sign of recent occupation.

Otherwise, the interior seemed built to no sensible design. Bedrooms opened off the stairs seemingly at random, and large sections were walled off with no sign of any means of entry to the space that must exist behind the walls. In one case, the door into a bedroom was a foot above the floorboards, as though floor and doorway were built at different times.

When they returned to the kitchen, Pat had cleared up the worst of the mess, and stood by a barrel with a mug of beer in his hand.

"Your uncle has good taste in beer, miss," he said as Hope descended the steps.

William followed her through the door above. "And you, Pat, are supposed to be helping, not drinking. Fetch coal from the pile outside, so Mrs Phillips can cook."

An hour later, Hope and William sat in the kitchen with cups of hot tea. Eliza rested in a bedroom that Mrs Phillips had cleaned. Mrs Phillips now hummed to herself as she washed the old linen Howard had piled into one of the closets.

"This house is as strange as Uncle Howard," Hope said. "When do you think it could have been built?"

"No time I recognize," William said. "It is a monstrosity."

Hope would hardly disagree. If she had seen it from the path while passing by, she would have given it as wide a berth as the villagers had suggested.

That the raven-haired girl in the village said she had been brave enough to enter the house all alone after walking along the cliffs from the village told Hope that she would have made a fine wife for Uncle Howard if he had wanted one.

If he ever returned, perhaps she still would.

Hope sipped from her cup. The warm liquid was welcome after the long, cold trip. Thuds and grunts echoed down the stairs from above as Pat finished his cleaning work, carrying water from the well, and preparing fires and lanterns to get them through the first night in the house, until he could unpack the cart.

Of Howard himself, they had found no sign other than his keyring. The house had been deserted for days, and Howard had left no indication of why he left, or where he might have gone. He had certainly done his best to ensure no-one would enter while he was away, as though he had left for an extended time.

"Perhaps a letter crossed paths with us," William said. "It may be waiting when we return home."

"If he left to travel, why would he leave his dog behind, with only kitchen supplies to eat? And why would he go to such trouble to secure the house, then leave a set of keys loose in the garden?"

"I agree that his behaviour seems unusual, but Howard has always been unusual, doubly so since he returned from India."

She couldn't disagree with that. If he had been sick at the time, then his behaviour might have been more unusual than was usual even for him.

"Do you think, perhaps, that his disease returned from the Orient with him?"

"Some are known to upset the mind. It would not surprise me if that had caused him to behave in such a strange way."

"Shall we return to London?"

Hope waited expectantly for the response. Every day away from her Herbert was a day too long. Surely they couldn't wait around for Howard forever?

"No. We shall stay in the house for the summer. Howard will return when he sees fit."

"Father, you should not leave the business unattended for so long. You know they need you."

"I have left it in good hands. They can manage to run it for one summer."

"But Father..."

"No. I know why you wish to return, and it has nothing to do with my business. The break will do us all good, particularly you and your mother."

"We do not even know that Howard is still alive, let alone that he will return."

"If he does return, we will be here to greet him. If not, then in the autumn we will seal the house as we found it, and return home. We will not leave before."

That would keep her apart from Herbert for months. Couldn't she think of a better excuse to return early?

"What about Kerberos?"

"I am sure Howard will understand if we choose not to leave Kerberos behind to fend for himself again."

On hearing his name, Kerberos looked up from a bowl of water on the floor. He had been working hard to quench his appetite and thirst since Mrs Phillips laid out some food and water for him. By the amount he drank, he would probably not have lasted much longer if they hadn't found him.

"How are we for supplies, Mrs Phillips?" William said.

"The dog left plenty for us, sir. At least when combined with those we brought from the village."

William nodded and sipped his tea. "We will try to replace them before we leave if Howard does not return."

"What about the house? It is in a great mess."

"I will retain Pat for now to look after the horses and the house. We can send him to the village for supplies, if we must."

He leaned closer to Hope.

"You are not to be alone with him at any time. I do not like the way he treats you."

Hope nodded rather than argue. No man had ever treated her quite that way before. Herbert wouldn't be happy if he heard that she showed any interest in another man.

Footsteps thumped down the stairs, and a lantern's glow swung across the walls as Pat descended.

"Your uncle has planks, nails and tools in a shed by the stables," he said. "Though he must have used a lot of it on the house before he left."

"You can use the rest to make repairs," William said.

"When I've finished washing, miss," Mrs Phillips said, "I'll make some hot water so you can have a nice bath."

Hope stretched. "There are few things I'd like more than a warm bath and a warm bed, after that trip."

Pat nodded toward her. "Wouldn't mind joining you, miss."

"Pat..." William said.

Pat wriggled his shoulders "Oh, sorry, sir. I meant, I wouldn't mind a nice warm bath myself. All this carrying makes my arms ache."

"I believe I know what you meant."

"I should finish sorting out the fires."

"Yes, I think you should."

William wound all the clocks in the study, then reset them to the correct time according to his watch. Hope examined Howard's library in the study bookcase as she waited for Mrs Phillips to fill the bath. Even the names of the books on the spines were written in foreign characters, and the interiors of most were little but squiggles and pictures. More of Howard's souvenirs from his time abroad?

She pulled down a book with a thick, dark leather cover. The text was just squiggles, but she flipped through pictures of creatures that couldn't exist on God's Earth. Wings, horns, tentacles, bodies that seemed made of bone, faces covered with thousands of eyes, teeth the size of shovels. Surely even India and Africa couldn't hold such monstrosities?

Many of the creatures seemed to spend their time chasing naked girls. She thought back to the words of the blacksmith in the village. Could there be any truth to his comment about Howard giving girls to demons?

She flipped to a drawing of a creature with a goat's head, tentacles and what appeared to be a fat marrow between its furry, hoofed legs. It was chasing after screaming girls, who wore little but scraps of torn cloth.

William glanced over her shoulder at the book, then took it from her hands and slammed it shut.

"I have told you that you are to read nothing but the Bible. I do not know where Howard found these books, but they are not the kind a young lady should be reading."

"Ezekiel 23," Hope said, a story she had studied on the trip. "There were two women, the daughters of one mother, and they committed whoredom in Egypt..."

"Stop that," William said.

He pushed her toward the open door, then put the books in the bookcase and locked it. He ushered her from the study, then locked the door.

"You are not to enter there again. Howard will be unhappy if you interfere with his possessions."

With the outside door locked too, there was no way in. There must be a clue to Howard's disappearance in the books he was reading. Besides, part of her wanted to know what happened to the girls after the creature caught them.

"Yes, father," she said. She'd find another way, somehow.

Hope curled up in bed after her bath, and a dinner of bread, and whatever meat and vegetables Mrs Phillips had found in the kitchen to cook in a stew.

"Howard has quite a gun collection in the study," William had announced as he dipped into the stew. Indeed, that seemed to be the only luxury Howard had allowed himself in his seclusion, other than the books. "I plan to teach Henry how to shoot while we are here. It should help pass the time, and will be a useful skill."

Eliza had ignored him as she stirred her spoon in the stew. Henry, on the other hand, was delighted. Hope didn't even ask if she could join, as he wouldn't consider such behaviour to be seemly for a young lady, either.

She sat in bed, writing her journal, trying to record as much as possible of the events of the day. The candlelight flickered across the page, and her eyes struggled to focus on the paper. She rubbed them, then walked to the window for some fresh air. She peered between the curtains, at the view of the sea by starlight, the moon high in the sky and only just past new.

As she looked out, the surroundings seemed brighter than expected from such dim lighting. She leaned out of the window and looked down, to see whether a light was still lit in one of the rooms below her.

All the windows were dark, and, as her eyes adjusted, she realized where the light was coming from.

The house glowed.

CHAPTER FOUR

In the morning, Hope strolled through the yard to the stable. Mrs Phillips had fully adapted to their temporary home, if the size of the morning's breakfast was anything to go by. After they finished eating, William took Eliza upstairs and read to her, leaving an opportunity for Hope to explore further. She would take a ride on the moors, and hunt for any sign of Uncle Howard.

Pat had cleaned the tack Howard left in the stable, and was repairing the doors and walls when she reached it.

"Busy, I see, Pat," Hope said.

"That I am, miss. With all the work to do around here I reckon I'll be staying with you for some time."

The stallion twisted, turned and whinnied in his stall, and didn't seem happy to be there.

"Saddle one of the horses for me," Hope said.

"I'm here for whatever you desire, miss," Pat said.

She looked out over the grounds as Pat worked. The moor between the house and village was desolate and windswept, with little sign of life beyond grass, bushes and the occasional tree. Even Howard's estate had only a few bushes and trees between the house and the stunted woods. How long could she go without the sight of green grass and tall trees of London's parks?

Pat led one of the mares from the stable, and handed the reins to her. As he did so, he briefly held her hand in his. Hope pulled on the reins, and her hand slid free of his fingers. The look in his eyes said it was no chance occurrence.

She had been forgiving of him the previous day, but a good night's sleep had made her think again. He wasn't a man she could call handsome, the way Herbert's military manner made him handsome. But he was rugged and muscular in the way of these rural folks, and some would surely find him so.

He held out his hands, and helped her into the saddle.

"Fine legs, miss."

Hope glared down at him.

"I meant the horse, miss."

Should she say anything to her father? Perhaps his view of Pat's attentions was justification enough to encourage them. She pressed her leg against the horse's side and tapped the other with her whip, then twisted the reins to lead it out of the yard.

"Don't get lost, miss," Pat yelled after her.

She rode to the north-east of the house, following the dark wall beside the twisted trees of the wood. If only Herbert rode beside her, she would have appreciated the company, and he would have appreciated riding through the rough countryside more than she did.

Who could have built a monstrous estate in such a remote location? The cost must have been tremendous, and the strange black stone used to build the wall was unlike any she had seen before. The wall appeared to be a single, solid block of stone, which glowed at night. It was as though the black stone was part of the cliff, and the house and wall were carved from it.

After quarter of a mile, the sound of hooves approached from behind her. Pat trotted toward her on the stallion. She stopped to wait for him.

"And what brings you out this way, Pat?"

"Didn't seem right to let you ride out here on your own, miss. We still don't know what happened to your uncle, and anything could happen to you. Mr Hodges would have blamed me if it did, so I thought I'd better come and protect you."

She let him ride beside her, keeping her mare a safe distance from his stallion, and they continued along the narrow strip of land between wall and wood. Old, worn hoof-prints crossed the dirt there, but of Howard there was no sign.

Pat pulled closer, and the stallion's head twisted toward the mare. "Doesn't seem the sort of place for a lady like you, miss."

"What do you mean?"

"You don't seem the country type. Nor your parents."

"I believe Father is punishing me. He feels I was becoming too close to one of his old friends, a cavalryman whom Howard introduced us to some years ago."

"Ah, you shouldn't trust soldiers, miss. They'll say anything to get a girl in bed, then go looking for another as soon as they get out of it."

"Herbert is a Captain in the Royal Lancers, not a common Private chasing a camp follower. His wife died in childbirth two years ago, and he has been a widower since."

"Your father does seem protective of you, miss."

"I am sure Father is only concerned for his reputation. He cares a hundred times more for Henry than for me. If we had eloped together he would never have lived it down."

Pat nodded. "Ah, one of my friends wanted to elope with his girl, miss."

"And he did not?"

"Oh, he met her outside the house all right, and said he was relieved, because he thought she'd never get the rope out the window to climb down. She said 'I thought that too. I'd never have managed if my dad hadn't been so eager to help'."

Hope smiled at his joke. Then shrieked as the mare stumbled and threw her from the saddle.

As she lay on the ground, her breath knocked from her by the fall, Pat climbed down and helped her to her feet, then checked her mare's leg.

"Is she all right?" Hope said.

"Looks like it, miss." He pointed toward a deep depression in the ground. "Must have caught her hoof in that and tripped."

"What is that?"

"Could be from an old smugglers' tunnel, miss. Used to be lots on the coast around here, most haven't been used in years, and they collapse if they're not kept in good order."

The mare seemed no worse for her experience. Pat helped Hope back into the saddle, and they continued their horseback tour of the estate. This time watching for any sign of weak ground ahead. The gap between the wood and wall narrowed until it became too narrow to pass, and the top branches of the trees reached over the wall. The only choice was to turn around and retrace the steps to the house.

After lunch, Pat helped William set up the croquet outside the study. The rough grass was barely worthy of being called a lawn, and hardly suited for croquet with its bumps and holes. Hope watched a rabbit watch them from its burrow by a tree as they worked.

William had been intrigued by the game since they saw it at the Great Exhibition, and, at least, it was one more way to pass the days while they waited. As Hope imagined the long days of summer with only her family and the Bible for company, she could think of no more pressing concern than finding things to fill the time.

Henry had taken as enthusiastically to croquet as he did to anything else, but his enthusiasm didn't translate into success. William was doing his best to help him, which Hope wouldn't mind if his method wasn't to hinder her.

William and Mrs Phillips led Eliza toward a chair outside the house.

"Where is Howard?" Eliza said. Other than asking that six times a day, she had shown little interest in anything since they arrived.

"He will come back soon," William said, and helped her into the chair. "Meanwhile, some sun and fresh air will do you good."

Mrs Phillips sat in the chair alongside, the clacking of her knitting needles taking the place of conversation. William handed out the croquet mallets and balls, then dropped his on the grass. "May the best man win."

Pat returned to his task of repairing the windows by the study as they played, but spent more time studying Hope. Was he seriously pursuing her, or had the arrival of someone with more prospects than the village girls aroused his interest? His gaze caught hers as she lined up a shot, and she looked away.

She swung the mallet and knocked her croquet ball through a hoop. Henry lined himself up with the hoop, swung, and hit his ball with what strength he had, but he had never been a strong boy, or a particularly healthy one. It hit the hoop and bounced off.

William was coming last in the game and hit his ball through the previous hoop, coming to a stop close to Hope's. She then hit hers straight through the next hoop, taking the lead from Henry.

"Is Mother all right?" Hope said.

"Your mother is just upset from the strain of the journey," William said. "The air here is so much cleaner than London, it can only improve her health."

Henry then had an easy shot as his ball was only a few feet from the hoop, and it rolled through and stopped just behind Hope's.

William prepared to take his shot. At first he aimed at the hoop to follow the others, but, instead of swinging his mallet, he changed his aim and knocked Hope's ball well out of the way with his, leaving Henry in the lead.

"Father, that is not fair," Hope said.

"All is fair in war and croquet, my dear. Besides, you are in the lead, who else should I try to stop?"

She took careful aim on her ball before swinging the mallet, and it reached the hoop, only to hit the side and bounce back. Henry was already waiting for his chance, and his ball went through.

William clapped. "Well done, my boy."

Hope could have hit her ball straight through the hoop with ease, but William knocked it out of the way again, right into the flowerbed. She knocked it hard toward the hoop, hitting the side again, but this time going through.

"Then why has Mother barely come out of her room?"

"You cannot expect her to improve in such a short time," William said. "Mrs Phillips will give your mother her medicine until she brightens up."

Did he really believe that? The tone of his voice didn't match the words.

Henry was still in the lead, but not by much. He hit his ball to the final hoop but not hard enough. It stopped before going through.

William lined up to hit his ball, aiming at Hope's. As he swung his mallet, she took her chance both to ask a question she had wanted to ask, and to distract him from the shot.

"Are you sure that's all that's wrong with her?"

His head jerked up at the question, and the mallet hit the ball on the side. It rolled past Hope's.

"I am sure she is also upset about Howard's disappearance," he said. "You would be too, if Henry disappeared with no in-dication of where he had gone, or even whether he was alive. She will recover in time."

"If Henry was to disappear, I would go looking for him, not hide in my room."

"Your mother is not as pig-headed as you, my dear."

Henry took his shot, knocking his ball through the hoop.

"Did I win?"

"Not quite," William said. "Remember the rules we taught you."

Hope studied the balls on the grass. She could easily knock William's right off the lawn. But that would just fall into his plan. She aimed for the hoop.

"And if you continue to show an interest in Pat," William said, "you will be confined to your room."

Her mallet hit the ball, which hit the hoop and bounced off.

She glanced at Pat, who was keeping one eye on her as he worked. "I have no interest in Pat. "

William lined up his mallet and hit his ball. His hit hers, and knocked it into the flowerbed.

"Can we not just find Howard and return home?" she said.

"Your turn, Henry," William said. "If we knew where Howard might be, we could go looking for him. For all we know he could have travelled back to India. Meanwhile we can do little but wait and hope that he returns."

"I won! I won!" Henry shouted. They looked around and saw his ball resting against the centre stake. He had won, but only because William had decided Hope should lose.

William clapped. "You should not worry whether you win or lose, my dear, just enjoy the game."

He walked to Henry, congratulated him on his victory, then picked him up and carried him toward the house.

Pat looked over from the ladder, where he was replacing a pane of glass in the study window. "Ay, has anyone seen my hammer?"

William shook his head. "Afraid not."

"I was sure I left it on the ladder not five minutes ago."

William strode into the house with Henry. Pat watched Hope as she followed them.

"Better luck next time, miss."

Eliza soon retired to bed, and with nothing more exciting to do, Hope climbed the stairs to her room. She would have knocked, but she didn't think Eliza would respond either way. Hope opened the door and looked in. Eliza was sitting in the bed, staring at the window.

Hope stepped into the room and closed the door behind her, then sat on the bed.

"What are you doing?" Hope said.

Eliza looked at her, but said nothing.

"Is there anything I can get you?"

Eliza lay back against the headboard, showing no interest in Hope's visit or anything else. Hope stood.

"Where is Howard?" Eliza said.

"We have been looking for him."

"I would like to talk to Howard when he returns. We have much to discuss."

That would be a pleasant change after her recent silence.

"I will tell him," Hope said.

Eliza turned to look toward the window. Was Hope now dismissed? Her mother showed no more sign of interest, and Hope returned downstairs.

Henry sat in the kitchen with Kerberos and Mrs Phillips. He seemed to have taken to the dog, who sat with his tail wagging while Henry scratched under his chin.

"Henry," Hope said, "you should not be playing down and here bothering Mrs Phillips."

"He's not being a bother, miss. He's been helping me cook."

"I am sure he has better things to do."

"We are making eel pie," Henry said.

Mrs Phillips laid a lump of pastry on a board, and pressed it down with her fingers. "Kerberos here ate most of the salt meat, but didn't seem to think much of the smoked eel. Mr Hodges says he and Pat will shoot us a deer, later."

"Father is going to teach me to shoot," Henry said. "Perhaps I can go with them."

"I do not think he would want to risk anyone accidentally shooting you out in the woods," Hope said.

She didn't add that he wouldn't want Henry to accidentally shoot anyone else, either. Between Henry's enthusiasm and inexperience, that was probably the greater threat.

Mrs Phillips rolled out the pastry. "Perhaps you can find us some hares. I have some good recipes for hare."

Henry pulled a cloth bag from his jacket pocket and held it out. "Let's play marbles."

"I have other things to do," Hope said.

Henry pulled the marbles from the bag. "Come on."

"We will be in Mrs Phillips' way while she cooks."

Mrs Phillips slapped the pastry in a pie dish. "You're not causing any harm. I'd appreciate the company."

Hope would rather continue exploring the estate, but Henry was already chalking a circle on a stone floor beside the table. She crouched beside him to play.

"Pat said he would take me riding," Henry said.

"I am not sure that would be a good idea."

"Why not?"

"Until we find Uncle Howard, who knows what dangers might lurk around the estate?"

Hope had never been good at the game, so they were evenly matched, and continued until Mrs Phillips' pie was ready for supper, and concluding with a solid draw.

She returned to her room, to change for dinner. Eyes watched her from the shadows near the foot of the stairs. Pat stood there with a smile on his face, staring at her.

"Good evening, Pat," she said.

"Evening, miss."

He stepped in front of her, holding his hands behind his back. Her heart thudded and her body shivered. What was he waiting there for? If the man decided to take his interest further, could her father do anything to stop him?

"Please move aside," she said. "I am going to my room."

As she tried to step past him, he brought his hands around in front of his chest. He raised a bunch of flowers toward her.

"I brought these for you, miss. Thought they might cheer you up after your game out there."

She took them. The long, ridged stems and red petals were unfamiliar, but they could be another souvenir Howard had brought back from overseas. Hopefully he wouldn't mind that Pat had picked them.

"Thank you," she said. "But I am not sure Father would think kindly of you for doing so."

He smirked at her, then stepped aside so she could pass.

"Your dad doesn't need to know, now does he?"

She filled a vase with water and placed the flowers beside her bed. Should she even have accepted his gift? At least if it kept William from becoming complacent, it may be of some benefit.

CHAPTER FIVE

Hope knelt in the lounge after dinner, her head bowed and palms together. Eliza knelt beside her in silence, and Henry knelt beside Kerberos on the far side, his eyes twitching toward the dog when they were supposed to be closed.

"And we pray for Uncle Howard," William said. "That, wherever he may be, God will look over him."

"Amen," Hope said.

"Amen," Henry said, as he scratched Kerberos' chin.

Eliza crossed herself.

The windows shook, and a flash illuminated the lounge as lightning flashed outside. Thunder rumbled, and rain splattered on the glass.

William slapped his Bible shut and placed it on the table. "Time for bed."

An hour later, Hope still lay awake in her room, listening to the rain lashing against the windows and the lightning crashing along the coast. Every time she closed her eyes, the thunder rumbled outside, and the rain thudded so hard on the windows that the house could surely not stand much longer?

Perhaps the storm was a sign that God was unhappy with Uncle Howard. They were lucky the weather had remained good until they reached the house, because she wouldn't want to have ridden through that on the cart.

She peered out of the windows. Puddles filled every low spot in the garden, and the leaves of the bushes and trees swung in the wind, their wet surface reflecting the light from the moon and the house.

If only Herbert was there to keep her warm, and comfort her when the lightning flashes made her jump.

A bush at the edge of the garden swung more than the others, and a dark shape moved behind it. Was it an animal, or could Howard be watching them from down below? He would have to be madder than usual to hide outside in this weather.

The door banged behind her. She glanced toward it as the handle twitched and the key rattled in the lock.

"Who is it?" she called.

The rattling stopped. Was it Pat? Howard? Her father come to check she wasn't up to no good? Or just thunder shaking the house?

She waited a moment, then opened it and looked out onto the landing. The moon cast only a dim pool of light through the window, and only faint shadows showed outside it.

She closed the door and locked it, then looked out of the window again. The dark shape was gone, and the bushes blew in the wind.

She awoke in the morning. The rain had slowed to a patter on the glass, and a beam of sunlight shone through her window from a gap between the grey clouds.

Pat's flowers were brown and wilted. They had gone from fresh to long dead in a few hours. They had plenty of water in the vase to sustain them. Could something in the water have poisoned them? Was it safe to drink? What if Howard had poisoned himself drinking from the well? She could ask Pat, but he might be upset that she had killed his gift.

She carried them downstairs, intending to throw them into a remote part of the garden while Pat was otherwise occupied. Instead, she met William as he was leaving Eliza's room.

"Where did those come from?" he said.

"Pat gave them to me," she said. William stared at her with a furrowed brow.

"They looked fine last night," she added. "Do you think the water here killed them?"

He took the vase from her. "If they were not dead, I would have thrown them out myself. That man is a common labourer, for God's sake. A drunkard. And a Catholic. You caused enough trouble for this family in London, I will not see you throwing yourself at a man like that."

"I am not throwing myself at anyone."

"Just because we are away from London, that is no excuse for you to go native. I realize you are troubled by your mother's sickness, but when we return home we will find you a husband who is suited to your station."

"Father. I have met those men, and they bore me to tears."

"Do not believe I will not confine you to your room if you disobey me."

She pulled a flower from the vase and pretended to sniff it. "Grandfather was a farm labourer."

"And he is dead and you will not speak of him again. I should never have let him put his mad ideas into your head."

With that, he took the flower from her, and stormed down the stairs. Eliza joined them for breakfast, but she showed little more interest in eating than talking.

"Where is Howard?" she said.

"How is your breakfast?" William said.

Eliza opened her mouth to speak, then looked down at her plate. She silently chopped a fried egg into smaller and smaller pieces until it became a mass of white and yellow.

"Mrs Phillips even found fresh mushrooms," William said.

They were fried on the plate, and a decent breakfast seemed to have raised Henry's spirits, if not Eliza's. He chopped the end from a sausage, then tossed it onto the floor for Kerberos.

"Where is my brother?" Eliza said.

"Howard has left for a while," William said. "He will soon be back."

"When will that be?"

Mrs Phillips poured tea as William sliced his bacon. "Very good breakfast, Mrs Phillips. Very good."

"I do my best, sir," Mrs Phillips said.

Eliza leaned over the table toward William. "I must speak to Howard."

"You can, when he returns."

Hope ate her breakfast in silence as Eliza asked about Howard, and William tried to avoid her questions. Her mother had done her best to keep the children away from Howard since his last visit when Hope was young. What could be so important that she suddenly wanted to talk to him about?

Continuing her own search for Howard would give Hope something to do. Besides, Henry was eager to explore, and the others would be better off without him under their feet.

Kerberos joined the expedition, and they walked to the far end of the garden, past the apple trees whose few apples mostly lay rotting on the ground after the storm had blown them from the branches. The further from the house they progressed, the further the gardens regressed, until they were pushing their way between the low bushes and peculiar ferns.

Then the ground fell away ahead of them. Hope grabbed Henry's shoulder to stop him falling as she looked down. A pit had been dug in the ground, forty feet long and twenty or more feet deep. The dirt from the hole was piled alongside, and looked quite fresh, with only a few patches of grass and weeds growing upon it.

Henry pulled away from her, and pushed through the bushes to the far side. He found a rough wooden ladder and placed a foot on it to climb down.

"Henry, stay out of there," Hope said.

He ignored her, and laughed as he hurried down the ladder. She strode around the pit, and reached the ladder at the same time as Henry jumped down the last few rungs onto the dirt floor. Kerberos leaned over the top of the ladder and peered in.

"Henry, hurry up and come back."

He glanced back at her, then walked around the bottom of the pit, kicking at the dirt. Then he crouched and began to dig.

"What have you found?" she said.

He ignored her and continued to dig. Climbing down to join him would be almost impossible in her dress.

Henry stood, turned and held something in his hand.

"Look at this."

Hope swung her parasol to shade her eyes from the sun. Henry held a bone in his hand, what looked like a jaw with long teeth, some of them missing. Then he dug deeper in the dirt, exposing more white beneath the brown.

"There's more, too," he yelled.

"Henry, put that down."

"I'm going to show Father."

"Henry, you are not going to dig up old bones and take them to Father. He has more important things to do."

Henry grabbed one of the teeth between his fingers and wiggled it until it came free. He held it up, the sharp edges shining in the sunlight.

"Besides," Hope added, "You could catch something from it. This could be how Howard became sick."

Henry studied the bone again, then nodded and dropped it.

"Now, come back up. We have more exploring to do."

He strode back and climbed the ladder. As he approached the top, Hope crouched and took hold of his arm in case he fell.

They passed more pits as they continued their stroll to the south, this time Henry content to stay by her side. If Howard had dug them, he must have spent most of his time doing so. Was he constructing something, or looking for something?

Beyond the pits, the ground was level for a hundred yards before it dropped away into a ravine, where in places the slope was shallow enough to descend without risk. As they reached the bottom, Henry sat on a rock beside a fast-flowing stream that ran through it. He began to untie his shoes.

"What are you doing?" Hope said.

He pulled off his shoes, then his socks, and pushed the socks into the shoes. Then he handed them both to her.

"I'm going paddling."

Hope carried the shoes as he pulled up his trouser legs and splashed his feet in the stream.

"Do not get cold," she said. "Mother will not want you at home sneezing all day."

He ignored her, and splashed down the stream as fast as he could run. Further along the ravine, the undergrowth grew thicker, with bushes and small trees replacing long grass. If William was correct, perhaps the high ravine walls helped to protect them from the wind.

"Henry, wait," she yelled, but held little hope of him doing anything she asked. She could hear him laughing and splashing ahead. She pushed her way through the bushes to follow the river, and found him throwing stones into the water, while Kerberos chased the splashes.

"Let us follow the ravine to the end, or as far as we can," she said, and took Henry's hand, so she would have some chance of keeping him under control. As they moved toward the sea, the walls became steeper as the ravine widened and deepened.

Then, as they pushed through a patch of tall bushes and low trees, the stream opened out into a large pool. On the far side of the pool, the stream continued down toward the sea, and the ravine narrowed again.

"Hello, miss," Pat yelled as he swam in the pool, his bare tanned skin visible through the blue water, and his clothes piled upon the rocks with a fishing rod lying across them.

Was he was there for his own reasons, or had he chosen to ambush them? Hope lowered her eyes as he turned toward her, then glanced his way again. Partly from fear that he might step naked from the water, partly from hope that he would.

"Will I find you everywhere I go?" she said.

He smirked and nodded. "I hope so, miss."

She couldn't think ill of the man. She found herself smiling back at his words, which contained all the good humour she had faked in hers. Perhaps, living so remote from civilization, he just had no idea how civilized people behaved.

"Does Father know you are here?"

"Mr Hodges lent me the rod, miss. He reckons there's good fishing in the stream, and Mrs Phillips will do wonders for us with fresh fish."

"And what are you fishing for at this moment?"

"I reckon I might have caught it, miss."

His brown legs moved beneath the clear water as he stepped forward in the pool until his chest rose out of it. Dark hair showed beneath the ripples, and something long and pink dangled below it.

She turned away, her heart thumping and body quivering. She wanted to see what was hidden below the water, but not for him to know that. She should turn and run back to the house, and tell her father to dismiss him, but she couldn't. In London, she wouldn't give him a second glance, but in this lonely and desolate house..? With her father concentrating on her mother, she had no acceptable companions besides Henry and Mrs Phillips. Summer alone would be Hell itself.

"Come on in," Pat said.

"Let's go swimming," Henry said.

Before Hope could respond, he had already removed his shirt, and begun to remove his trousers.

"Henry, stop that. You will catch a cold," Hope said.

He ignored her and jumped into the pool. Kerberos splashed into the water behind him.

"Come on, miss," Pat yelled.

"I am in no way prepared to join you," Hope said. "Even if I had a bathing dress, Father would not allow me to swim in a pool with," she hesitated, "a naked man."

She turned back to watch Henry, to ensure he came to no harm in the water, and turned her parasol so it blocked some of the view. Pat turned his body sideways, but she could still see hints of things under the water that her father wouldn't want a girl to see. Seeing Herbert without a chaperone had angered him, when Herbert was fully dressed. Henry was unlikely to qualify as one, and Pat was naked.

Pat splashed water towards her. "Ah, you don't need any fancy dress. Just whip it off and jump in, like the rest of us."

She smirked. "If Father heard I had 'whipped it off', he would be sure I had scandalized London society for the next century."

"From what Mrs Phillips said, miss, it seemed like you'd done that already."

"Mrs Phillips should not be spreading gossip."

"Well, what else does she have to keep her busy?"

Plenty, she would have thought, but there must be time enough for gossip between cooking and cleaning.

The water looked deeper than Hope had imagined, almost up to Henry's chest, even where he stood near the edge. He waded deeper and began to swim around the centre.

Pat motioned toward her. "Just come in. You know you want to."

He floated in the centre of the pool, raising ripples as his arms and legs moved under the water. Kerberos swam past, and Pat tried to grab his tail.

She could remove her boots and paddle in the water, but Henry had shown it was too deep for that, even near the edge. Besides, that would be enough of a scandal for her father. She settled for sitting on a rock and watching Henry as he swam.

"How deep is it?" she asked Pat.

"My feet can't touch the bottom."

"Then Henry should come out. If something happens, I cannot possibly rescue him."

Pat glanced at Henry, who giggled as he swam near the edge. "He'll be fine with me, miss."

Henry knew she had never learned to swim. William had taught him, but never taken the time to teach her. If the pool was much deeper than Henry was tall, there was no way she could possibly reach him. Perhaps that was Pat's intention, to encourage Henry into the pool where she would have to strip off to drag him out. Her father would never forgive her if she allowed Henry to come to harm.

Mrs Phillips' voice echoed around the ravine. "Pat? How's the fish coming?"

"Won't be long," Pat yelled. "I already got a couple."

He swam toward his clothes on the far side of the pool, then stood and walked out, naked. Hope did her best to look away again as he dressed, but glanced back just long enough to catch sight of his cock and balls swinging, smaller than they appeared in the water. He turned toward her, exposing his nakedness.

"Not seen a man naked before, miss?"

She looked away. For all her father's worries about Herbert, she had never seen him naked.

"It does not seem much of a thing to see."

"Ah, that's just the cold water, miss," he said, "Now I've got to be getting to work."

"Then you are coming out too, Henry."

Henry laughed. "No, I am staying here. If you want me, you will have to come and get me."

Pat picked up his fishing rod.

"'Bye, miss," he said, then wandered upstream.

"Good luck with the fish," Hope called after him. He glanced back at her over his shoulder, before he disappeared into the undergrowth.

"Henry," she said, "there is a special place in Hell reserved for boys who disobey their sisters."

He continued to laugh and swim. She could wait for him to tire of swimming, or get him out of the pool herself.

"I am not coming in there for you," she said.

"Then I will stay here until I am bored."

She watched him as he swam in circles, Kerberos paddling along behind him. His body was already turning blue from the cold. If he caught cramp, she would have to watch him sink to the bottom of the pool and drown.

She removed her skirt, and, with difficulty, stripped down to her chemise. If only her clothing could be as easy to remove as Henry and Pat's. Goose-pimples rose on her bare skin as she stepped into the water from the heat of the sunlit ravine. Her whole body shivered as the icy temperature worked its way up her legs from her toes.

"Henry, do not make me come and get you," she said one last time. He ignored her, and she stepped in.

The cold water rose to her thighs, and she panted as it sucked the heat from her body. She would soon be as frozen as he was.

She stepped toward him and the water rose to her waist, then her chest. She paused and panted between steps, so her body would become accustomed to the cold. Henry floated twenty feet ahead, watching her with a smirk on his face.

"When I get you back to the house, I will tell Father about this."

"If you do, I will tell Father about you and Pat."

She took another step and stopped, glad that the water was barely any higher than before. "There is nothing between Pat and I. And Father will not believe you if you tell him."

"And that is what you said about Herbert," Henry said and ducked his head under the water. He rose up again, and sprayed water from his mouth.

With no better choices left, Hope lifted her leg, then swung it ahead, ready to take a big step toward Henry. Her foot sank through the water, going below the level where she expected it to stop.

She tried to pull back as she realized that the bottom of the pool had disappeared, but had leaned forward too far. A second later, she was splashing her arms in the water like a mad woman as she struggled to stay upright. But her body twisted around, her other foot left the ground, and she began to sink. The cold water closed over her head, and she felt herself descending into depths that would never end.

Her arms and legs flailed as she struggled to return to the surface, but it was receding from her, and the sunlight fading beyond the dark water. She held her breath, but her lungs ached to breathe out to relieve the pressure, and try to suck in fresh air that would never come.

The water churned around her, and she struggled harder as something grabbed her around the chest. She struggled against the grip of the hungry sea creature, and tried to knock it away. Then Henry's face appeared in the water. A moment later, her face broke into the air at the surface and she gasped for a breath she had imagined she would never see. Henry helped her back to the shallows, and followed her from the water as she strode to dry land.

They sat on the rocks, as Hope panted in the salty sea air to regain her breath and calm herself.

Henry whistled and Kerberos swam toward him, then he looked at her.

"You should learn to swim."

A bush moved on the far side of the pool, and Hope watched it as Henry tried to wipe the water from his legs. The movement stopped, then another bush began to shake.

Kerberos climbed out of the pool, and growled.

"What is that?" Henry said.

"Probably a deer," Hope said. Or was it something else?

She raised her voice. "Because if it was a man hiding there to spy on us, I believe he would get into great trouble with my father for doing so."

The movement stopped, then more leaves twitched in a bush further up the ravine. Whatever the prowler was, it had moved away.

Kerberos shook the water from his fur, then lay on the warm rock. They sat for a moment as the heat of the sun dried their skin and clothes, then dressed and continued their walk.

Finally, they reached the end of the stream. It ran to the cliff, and down a steep incline to the rocks below. A steep enough drop that Hope's head spun from the sight as she looked over the edge. What an exciting fall it would make, before her body smashed into the rocks and tumbled down to the water.

She stepped back, and grasped the nearest branch so she wouldn't fall.

"Let's climb down," Henry said.

He was certainly brave. Or, perhaps, stupid.

"No. We'd never get back up in time for tea."

He picked up a stone and threw it over the cliff, where it smashed against the rock a dozen or more times with loud cracks as it fell to the beach. Hope gripped the branch even tighter than before.

Rocks and soil fell from the edge of the ravine into the stream behind them. Kerberos barked at the rock fall and crept toward it, as though he had spotted some wild animal.

"Kerberos, stop," Hope said.

The incline could be treacherous, and must be unstable for pieces to fall that way. Howard would surely be unhappy if he returned to find his dog injured.

Henry picked up another handful of stones from the bed of the stream and began to throw them over the cliff.

"Be careful," Hope said, then stepped to where Kerberos sat, and looked where he was staring up the ravine. Nothing was moving, but he continued to growl. Could he smell something up there that she couldn't see?

"Pat?" she called. What could have caused the commotion other than the curious Irishman?

He didn't respond. If he was there, he must have climbed out of the ravine and followed them that way, then run back to his fishing when he accidentally caused the rock fall. She would have words with him when they returned to the house.

A stone bounced across the ground between Kerberos and Hope. Henry giggled behind them, with another stone in his hands ready to throw.

"Henry, this place seems unsafe. We should return to the house."

He threw the last of his stones over the cliff, then crouched down to pick up some more. Hope took his hand and pulled him to his feet. He grimaced as she led him away from the cliff. Kerberos, on the other hand, was still convinced that something lurked at the edge of the ravine. He stared that way, and his nose twitched as he sniffed.

"Kerberos, come on," Hope said.

The dog's head turned, as though following something moving up the ravine. He growled, deep in his throat.

"Kerberos," she said again. He ignored her, padding slowly back along the ravine.

Hope released Henry's hand and grabbed Kerberos' collar. More dirt fell as she pulled Kerberos back. She glanced over her shoulder. Henry laughed as he clambered up the incline beside them, his hands and feet digging deep into the soft dirt.

Hope opened her mouth to shout at him, but he would be just as likely to hurt himself coming back down as climbing up. Kerberos pulled away from her and climbed the incline himself, and Hope followed. By the time she reached the top, her boots, gloves and skirt were coated with dirt. As they walked back to the house, she looked for Pat, but saw no sign of him. Henry found a stick, and entertained himself by throwing it, while Kerberos calmed down, no longer looking for prowlers behind every bush.

They arrived at the house, and entered through the front doors, eyes slowly adjusting to the dim light in the hallway. But something was wrong.

The cellar door was open.

"Father?" Hope called.

He hadn't been outside, and Hope peered into the dining room and lounge, both of which were empty. Had he found his way into the cellar while they were outside?

"Can we explore the cellar while the door is open?" Henry said.

Sometimes Hope wished she shared his youthful lack of imagination. Who knew what could be down there?

But she wanted to know, even though she dreaded finding out just what Howard might have hidden behind a door that he had taken so much trouble to secure.

She found two lanterns and lit them, and they each carried one as they walked to the door. She held her lantern ahead of her and peered inside. A spiral stone staircase led into darkness below.

She stepped through the door, and began to descend the damp steps.

CHAPTER SIX

A hint of tobacco smoke in the air told Hope that her father had descended before them. She glanced back at the cellar door as she heard Henry's footsteps behind her. As well as the locks, tough metal plates and bars were screwed to the inside. Thick green moss grew between the stones of the steps, and grey and black mould was smeared across the walls.

Hope placed her foot on the next step, and yelled as it slid out from underneath her on the wet stone. She fell backward, her arm swung out, and she grabbed the door frame to steady herself.

"Be careful," Henry said.

After a brief pause to recover, she continued climbing down, slower than before. The last thing she needed was to crack her head on the steps.

"Who is that?" a voice called from below.

"Hope and Henry," Hope said.

For a moment she heard no response, and they continued to descend, their footsteps echoing back from the stone walls. Then William's voice called out again.

"Come on down, then, I suppose you might as well do something useful."

He stood at the bottom of the steps, holding his own lantern high above his head as he looked around the cellar.

"This place is very solidly built."

"How did you come down here?"

"I was looking through the study for any indication of where Howard might be. Instead, I found another keyring, and, when I tried it, I discovered one key fitted the cellar locks."

He held up the keyring. The keys had half a dozen prongs twisted at strange angles, unlike any Hope had seen before. Howard must have intended the door to stay locked.

Shafts of light shone down from tiny barred windows near the ceiling, a dozen feet above them. The windows cast small pools of light on the stone floor, while the rest of the cellar was dark. Viewed from the steps, even the light from the windows did little to illuminate the dark interior, as the cellar appeared to run the full length and width of the house, and numerous pillars reached from floor to ceiling to block the view.

"I wonder what Uncle Howard used it for?" Hope said. "And why are there bars on the door?"

"Perhaps he was trying to keep something out of here. You saw how he sealed the rest of the house. This would have made an excellent hidey-hole for him to defend."

That Howard felt a need for metal bars to keep something out of a locked cellar inside a barricaded house was worrying enough. But there was an even less palatable possibility.

"Or keep something in?"

"Perhaps he was worried by those smuggling stories. He might have locked it in case one of their tunnels opened up somewhere in the cellar. This house has been here a long time, and may well have seen other uses in the past."

Hopefully, he was right. But what might be hiding in the cellar if tunnels from the coast opened into it? If anyone could sneak in there without being seen or heard, they could have left anything hidden behind one of the pillars, or have made a home right below where the family were living.

They walked further into the cellar, and Hope tried to stay close to William for light and safety. The butt of one of Howard's revolvers poked from his jacket pocket, so he had clearly come prepared.

Something scratched in the darkness, and Hope swung the lantern around, illuminating a pile of wood. Light reflected back at her from a rat's eyes as it sat on its haunches, washing its face. It looked up and saw her, then dropped to all fours and vanished into the wood pile.

Hope walked onward, swinging the lantern in front of her as she peered into the darkness for any sign of other inhabitants. Large black rocks were piled against one wall, and she stopped to look at them.

She ran her hand over the irregular, shiny surface to wipe away some of the dirt and dust. The stones had been broken apart, and intricate patterns were carved around the edges which hadn't been broken. They appeared to be parts of one or more larger sculptures, as the edge patterns on several stones matched up. Whatever they had been, they were now in small enough pieces that she would need days to work out what the complete shape might be.

"What do you think these are?" she called to William.

He had found a rack of dust-covered wine bottles on the far side of the cellar, and was investigating them as intently as she was investigating her own find.

He walked to her and examined the rocks. "Basalt, perhaps? I believe that's common in this area."

"But the shapes? Surely they are not natural?"

He crouched and briefly examined them. "Perhaps Howard was trying to carve something while living alone here. He must have needed some hobbies to pass the time."

"He was digging huge holes in the garden. Perhaps this is what he was looking for."

"Or perhaps they are just rocks."

William led the way deeper into the cellar. They passed wooden planks stacked against the walls, and shelves holding lanterns and tinned food, plus gunpowder and other supplies for Howard's guns. That would be useful when William taught Henry to shoot.

Where was Henry? Hope looked behind them, but could see no sign of him in the darkness.

"Father, when did you last see Henry?"

William looked into the cellar behind them, and swung his lantern to light the shadows.

"Henry?" he called.

His voice echoed back from the wall and pillars. Was Henry hiding for his own amusement, or could something worse have happened to him?

William crept back toward the steps. Hope turned as she heard faint moaning from further into the cellar. Or was she just imagining it? Her heart thudded at the thought of Henry in distress, or a smuggler trying to entice her into the darkness.

She walked toward it, holding the lantern ahead of her.

Beyond the next pillar, more rocks stood by the walls, this time almost complete sculptures, most taller than her. A mix of human and animal heads, limbs, tentacles and other body parts combined into the strangest creatures she have ever seen. They reminded her of the drawings from the books in Howard's study, yet looked even less human. Had Howard sculpted them from the books, or brought them with him?

She heard the moaning again and turned from the sculptures to walk toward it. Something rattled ahead of her. She swung the lantern to look into the darkness.

"Father?" she said. "Henry?"

No answer from either.

"Pat?" Had he used the smugglers' tunnels to enter the cellar without their knowledge? The wine would entice him to visit, even if nothing else did.

Something clattered to the ground behind her. She swung around toward it, then backed away, even though that meant moving deeper into the cellar. Whatever it was, it was between her and the steps.

"Father!" she shouted toward the far end of the cellar.

Then a dark shape jumped toward her, howling. She tumbled backward and dropped the lantern, which smashed on the floor.

Henry's familiar laugh echoed around the cellar as he ran into the darkness.

"Henry!" she yelled after him. "What in God's name are you doing?"

A light moved in the distance, and William hurried toward her, carrying Henry's lantern as well as his own.

"What happened?" he said, as he took her hand and helped her to her feet.

Henry ran out again, from behind the nearest pillar. William turned at the movement, and Henry fell to the floor beside him. He stood, trying not to look guilty, but his lowered eyes showed everything William needed to know.

"Henry," William said.

"Yes, Father?"

"Go upstairs, and find your mother. She would appreciate some company."

"But Father..."

"Henry, do as you are told."

Henry took his lantern from William, then skulked toward the stairs. That was the first time William had reprimanded Henry since they arrived. He must have been concerned by the boy's behaviour.

"You should not have brought him," he told Hope. "And you should go with him. I do not want to have to worry about what might happen to you down here."

"No. I want to know what Uncle Howard was doing here. You are so busy looking after Mother, you cannot do everything yourself."

"I would rather you go upstairs and send Pat to assist me."

"If you want Pat down here, you can fetch him yourself. I am not leaving until I know what Howard hid here."

William said nothing. Hope brushed some of the dirt from her dress.

"Did you find anything of interest?" she said.

"No sign of Howard so far."

He swung his lantern, and continued toward the far end of the cellar with only the lantern and the light from the windows to guide them. They passed the accumulated possessions of past owners, piled up in trunks or leaning against the walls.

Numerous small alcoves led off into the cellar walls between the pillars. William stopped to examine shelves of old books in one of them. Hope found a candle on a shelf and lit it from his lantern, then walked to the far end of the cellar.

A large, solid, metal door was set in the far wall, and whatever was behind them must be outside the house. Hope pulled the handle, and the lock rattled but remained firmly shut. The many pronged keyhole seemed to be the same kind as Howard had used on the cellar door.

"Father," she called. "Come and look at this."

He tried each of the keys on the keyring, but none would open the door.

"I do not know what Howard might have been doing down here," he said, "but I am not sure that anyone should know."

The girl in the village had told Hope about horrible things Howard showed her. At the time, Hope thought she was just making it up, but now she could believe he had something to hide. That belief should have scared her, but only increased her curiosity.

They collected some of Howard's supplies, particularly those for his guns, and several bottles of wine. As they left the cellar, William locked the door, then dropped the keyring into his jacket pocket.

"Neither of you will go down there without permission."

CHAPTER SEVEN

Snow and ice covered the land like a thick white blanket. Hope still recognized the shape of Howard's estate, as though it had remained unchanged over whatever period of time had passed. Howard's house and the walls around the estate still stood, but the house was a column of the same black stone as the wall.

The last thing she remembered was lying in bed, kept awake by the cacophony of another thunderous storm. Had Pat's tales of smugglers' tunnels, and the strange sculptures in the cellar, inspired this dream?

Low buildings huddled, half-buried, in a circle across the snow-covered landscape, between towers even stranger than Howard's house. Beyond them, a tall circular building of the same glowing black stone rose high above its surroundings.

Lightning flashed in the sky above the alien city as Hope ran across the snow on all fours. Her body was grey and scaly, with sharp claws on her fingers and something heavy swinging between her back legs. She ran between the buildings toward a dark hole in the ice, which became a tunnel leading into the rock. The tunnel forked, then forked again, but somehow she knew which direction to run.

The tunnels seemed to go on forever, some tall and level, others narrow and vertical. She raced through them, her claws scrabbling for grip on the rocks, jumping across gaps where the sea water smashed against the walls of pits which descended far below. Left, right, up, down, something was calling to her, and she followed its call.

She threw herself from the end of a narrow tunnel, fell to a steep, inclined wall, and scrabbled down it to the floor below. In the centre of a tall cave, so wide the walls disappeared into the darkness before they reached the far side, sat conical creatures with many eyes near the point and tentacles around their base. High above them hung huge machines made of black stone that glowed like the house, compared to which the largest steam locomotive they had seen at the Exhibition would look puny, and which reminded her of some of the strange sculptures she had seen in the cellar. Lightning flashed and sparked between them, the light illuminating the cave and faint thunder echoing from the walls.

Many more of the grey-skinned creatures rushed around the caves, appearing and disappearing through more tunnels, some leading up toward the city, others deeper into the ground. They seemed to be working desperately at something, but she couldn't understand what. Had they moved down below to hide from the snow and ice until the weather improved?

The creature she inhabited grabbed rough hand-holds on the nearest wall, and used its claws to climb toward the ceiling. It swung from one rock outcropping to the next, and the view as it moved made her queasy as she looked down at the solid rock floor, far below. One mistake would be its last.

As she approached the machines, one of the creatures there turned and screeched at her. She screeched back, made a final swing, then threw herself toward a ledge around the machine. A bolt of lightning flashed past, and her body jerked as it hit her. She shrieked with pain, then found herself looking at the house from the wood as it currently existed, ice-free.

Then loud banging echoed around her head.

"Hope, breakfast," William's voice yelled through the door.

She dressed as quickly as she could, and raced to the dining room, wondering how she had invented such a world from the sights she had seen the previous day.

Eliza seemed happier, and dug into the solid meal that Mrs Phillips placed in front of her.

"You look better today, dear," William said.

"I spoke to Howard yesterday," Eliza said.

William and Hope glanced at each other. Was the apparent improvement really a deterioration of her condition, trading her old melancholy for madness? Or, perhaps worse, could Uncle Howard be hiding from them for some reason that made sense only to himself? What if he had been living in the cellar and sneaked out when they opened the door? Or still lived down there behind the locked door.

"Where is he?" William said.

"He was outside my bedroom window," Eliza said. "He is living below the house now, with others of his kind. He looked unwell, but claims he is healthy and seems content enough."

William nodded. "And what did you speak about?"

"Many things. He said this place is dangerous, and we should not be here."

"What kind of danger?"

"He said they are trying to save the city, and they have broken time, and that is why the clocks do not work. He said he joined them to study them, and is learning much about them."

Henry played with his knife and fork, holding them in his hands as though they were marching along the table. "Do not play with your cutlery," William said, as though his rules were more important than Eliza's sanity.

"What city?" Hope said.

"He did not say."

William leaned toward her. "I cannot imagine there was ever a city around here. Who would have built it? Or lived in it?"

"Perhaps Howard is staying at one of the villages?" Hope said. "Studying the locals?"

William motioned for Mrs Phillips to approach. "When Mrs Hodges has finished breakfast, take her back to her room and prepare more of her medicine. And tell Pat to fetch more coal."

Eliza said little else after her first strange revelation. Could Hope have imagined her dream in an instant at the dining table, or had she really dreamed of the city before her mother mentioned it? She still remembered the strange creature and frozen tunnels as though they were real.

Hope stepped into the kitchen, intending to ask Mrs Phillips if she had seen Pat. And there she found him, working his way through a plate of fish, and joking with Mrs Phillips.

"So the lady walks into the kitchen," he said, "and she smells tobacco smoke, so she looks in the coal cellar. Where she sees a soldier hiding among the coal. And so she says to the cook, 'I dismissed your predecessor for bringing soldiers to the house'. And the cook says..."

"He must be one she left behind, ma'am," Mrs Phillips said.

Pat laughed. "Ah, the old ones are the best, aren't they?"

Hope descended the steps. "Mrs Phillips, Mother is waiting for her medicine."

Mrs Phillips wiped her hands, waited for Hope to reach the kitchen, then climbed the stairs.

"So, Pat," Hope said. "Is there nothing else you should be doing than sitting in the kitchen?"

"I expect so, miss," he said, then proceeded to finish off a mug of beer.

"I want to go riding again. Prepare a horse for me, please."

He stood and approached her.

"What are you doing?" she said.

"I don't think that's what you really came down here for." He walked toward her, and stood just inches from her body. He was drunk, and his breath blew the smell of beer into her face. "Was it?"

"I do not know what you are suggesting."

He stepped toward her. She backed away, unsure whether he was right.

"I think you do," he said.

"I should call my father."

"If you did, he'd dismiss me."

She backed up further, until her dress pressed against the wall behind her. Pat stepped closer.

"He would, would he not?" Hope said.

He put his arms around her waist, pulling her toward him.

"But if he knew you had came looking for me, then he'd punish you, too."

He smirked as he released her, then wobbled up the stairs on drunken feet, leaving her wondering how serious his attentions might be. And what she should do about them. Her experience with Herbert, an officer and gentleman through and through, hadn't prepared her for a man who acted the way he did.

Perhaps that was why she couldn't prevent herself from tempting him.

Henry aimed and pulled the trigger. The shotgun barked, and thumped against his shoulder. A grey-white cloud of gulls and pigeons exploded into the sky as leaves shook from the impact of the shot. William took the gun from him and handed it to Pat to reload, then gave Henry the other.

Hope sat on the grass, safely behind Henry and out of range of the shot, reading her Bible. Kerberos lay beside her, sleeping calmly through the noise as though shooting had been a regular occurrence in his life. For once, Pat wasn't looking at her, which she confirmed by watching him over the top of her Bible.

He reloaded the first barrel, and had just started cleaning the second, when he looked up and caught her eye.

"Want to try, miss?"

William was still assisting Henry, trying to demonstrate the correct way to aim. She had done enough to encourage Pat that day, but she couldn't turn down the chance to do something more interesting than read. She stood, brushed dirt from her dress, and took the gun from him.

He held up a small, paper wrapped cylinder. "First, bite off the end of the cartridge," he said, and held it out to her.

She raised the paper to her mouth and bit down. It tasted of old fat and sulphur, and she grimaced as she pulled hard against her teeth, and tore the end off.

"Pour the powder into the barrel," he said.

He put his hand on hers, pushing the end of the cylinder into the barrel and shaking it. She glanced toward William, who was still looking in the opposite direction as he held up the other shotgun and instructed Henry on how to aim. Henry, meanwhile, watched them over his shoulder.

"Now roll the rest up," Pat said.

He took her hand in his as he showed her how to put the rest of the paper cartridge into the barrel. Something she could have worked out herself.

William handed his shotgun to Henry, who looked back at the tree and raised it to his shoulder.

"Now, we ram it in hard," Pat said as he pulled a metal rod from below the barrel and held it out to her. She pushed the rod into the barrel with his help, then pulled it out.

"Would have been more work if your uncle hadn't made up all these cartridges," Pat said. "It's like he expected to have to fight a war here."

"I imagine he learned the habit in the army. He fought through a few battles in his time abroad. If we ever find him, you can listen to all his war stories."

Henry fired at another bird, and scared it from the tree.

"Last, you stick the percussion cap on the nipple," he said as he turned the gun around. He handed her a cap and pointed at the place to push it on. As she did so, William turned and looked at them.

"Pat..." he said. For the first time, Pat seemed sheepish as he took the loaded shotgun by the barrel and turned to speak to William.

"Yes, Mr Hodges," he said.

William handed him the empty gun, and Pat handed him the one they had just loaded. William glanced at her, then stared at Pat.

"Stick to your job, Pat," William said.

Pat looked down as he replied. "Yes, Mr Hodges."

William handed the gun to Henry.

"Pat, go into the woods and see what you can scare up."

Pat slung the empty shotgun over his shoulder, nodded, and walked into the wood, stopping to break a small loose branch from one of the trees.

He swung the branch through the undergrowth as he walked along the edge of the wood. A bush shook as a bird flew out and up into the sky.

"Fire," William shouted.

Henry raised the shotgun and swung it toward the bird. He aimed carefully and pulled the trigger, but the bird flew on, less concerned by the shot than he was by the stick.

"Sorry, Father."

"Pat will find you another target."

Pat moved further into the wood, swinging the branch again at the bushes, and banging it against the tree trunks. Two more birds flew out.

Henry raised the shotgun and fired. This time a bird finally fell from the sky. It hit the ground with a distressing crunch, then pushed itself to its feet and struggled to move, dragging one wing behind it.

A smile spread across Henry's face as William slapped his back. "Well done. We'll make a shooter of you yet."

Then he took the empty shotgun from Henry, and handed it to Hope. "You can make yourself useful while Pat is busy."

She took the gun, and began to load it as Pat had shown her. Pat, meanwhile, was moving deeper into the wood in his hunt for more birds for Henry to scare or wound. He stopped, stared into the bushes, then crept forward.

He swung the stick hard. The bushes jerked as he hit them. Then something big and dark burst from the bush, slammed into Pat's chest and knocked him to the ground. Hope barely glimpsed it for a half second, before it vanished among the bushes and ferns, then raced deeper into the wood.

Without thinking, she dropped the gun and hurried to help Pat, but he was already climbing to his feet.

"What was that?" William said. "Did anyone see?"

Pat took Hope's hand, and, for once, she didn't mind. "Don't know, sir," he said. "I haven't heard of anything big loose out here, just a few deer."

"It's a deer!" Henry called and swung the shotgun toward the trees. "Can I shoot it?"

"Henry, no," Hope said. She had seen little of the creature, but she was sure that it wasn't a deer. It moved too fast, and more like a man than a beast.

William opened his mouth to speak. A loud crash and rumble interrupted him, and the ground shook beneath them for a moment. Kerberos finally woke, and shook himself as he climbed to his feet.

They turned toward the source of the noise. In the distance on the far side of the garden, a large column of dust rose into the sky.

CHAPTER EIGHT

As they watched the dust cloud rise high above the ravine, Hope realized Pat was still holding her hand behind her back, and twisted it free of his grip.

They walked toward the cloud, until they reached the edge of the garden, and looked down over the end of the ravine. A dozen or more feet of the cliff had collapsed where they had stood the previous day, so the stream no longer ran down a steep slope, and, instead, a waterfall dropped over the cliff edge to the rocks below. The area around it was covered with dirt, and dust floating in the air around them slowly coated their clothes.

"What could have caused that?" Hope said.

William lit his pipe and motioned toward the sea. "The ocean waves undermine the cliff at the bottom. After many years, the cliff collapses under the weight of the rock."

Henry pulled on her arm. "Can I go down there?"

"No," Hope said. "Even if you could climb down, it is not safe."

He turned to William instead. "Father, I want to go down."

"No-one is going down there until I am sure it is stable. Pat, take the guns back to the house. Henry has practised enough for one day."

Pat nodded.

"Oh, and Pat," William added. "Check the drain-pipe by our room, I heard it rattling in the storm. Then fetch more coal for Mrs Phillips."

"I can climb down," Henry said. "I am a good climber."

Hope stayed back from the edge of the cliff. Any closer and she could be carried down all the way to the sea, if the ground collapsed further. Not even Henry could safely find his way to the bottom of the steep drop now. Certainly, she couldn't.

"Stay away from here," William said, as Pat left. "More of the ravine could collapse before it stabilizes."

Henry leaned over the edge. "Please, let me go down."

Hope quickly grabbed his hand and pulled him away from the cliff, then ushered him back through the gardens toward the house. William stayed to survey the damage. Kerberos trotted along at their heels.

Henry picked up a stick which lay on the ground beneath one of the stunted apple trees. He turned and waved it toward Kerberos. "Kerberos, come here."

Hope slowed her pace, to ensure Henry didn't get too far behind. Kerberos jumped up at him and tried to bite the stick as Henry swung it around above his head.

"Fetch, boy," Henry shouted, then threw the stick back in the direction from where they came. The stick flew through the air, straight into the ravine. Kerberos barked at it, then ran to the edge of the ravine, and disappeared down the slope.

"Henry," Hope said. "You did that deliberately."

He just smiled at her, then laughed. When Kerberos didn't immediately reappear, Henry ran after him.

"Henry, Father told you not to go down there," she shouted.

"But Kerberos might get lost," Henry shouted back, then ran down the slope into the ravine.

If Henry got lost, or injured himself, Hope would be blamed. She followed them down.

By the time she reached the edge of the ravine, Henry was already at the bottom, by the stream. Kerberos was in the water, pushing his way between the bushes that grew across the stream, trying to grab the stick as it floated toward the sea.

Hope stepped onto the slope, holding the thin trunk of one of the stunted trees for support. Her foot slipped on the loose dirt, and she tumbled onto her back, with her feet beneath her as she slid down the slope.

As she slid to a stop by the stream, she pushed herself to her feet, and grimaced as a sharp pain ran through her right ankle when she put weight upon it. She followed Henry as fast as she could, hobbling along on her twisted ankle.

She pushed a bush aside and stepped through the gap. Henry was crouched low on the far side, and pointed across the stream.

"Look over there," he whispered.

Hope hobbled up behind him, and crouched to look over his shoulder so she could see what he was pointing at.

A tall bush.

"What am I supposed to look at?"

"There's something in the bush," he said, then picked up a stone from the stream, and threw it.

The stone hit the bush and rattled down to the ground through the branches. The bush twitched for a second, then stopped. More bushes moved further down the stream on the far side, as though something was creeping from one to the next, then all the movement stopped.

Then the bushes in front of them on their side of the stream moved, and a dark shape was visible in the shadows between the leaves. Pain forgotten for a moment, Hope stepped forward and pulled Henry toward her, as she tried to see what it was.

Then Kerberos ran out, holding the stick proudly in his mouth as his tail wagged behind him. Hope released Henry, who took the stick and threw it further down the ravine before she could stop him. Kerberos raced after it, and Henry ran on behind him. He broke a branch from one of the low trees, and strolled through the undergrowth, thumping the bushes and tree-trunks with the stick.

"Henry, don't do that."

"I want to find a deer, like Pat did."

"There are no deer in the ravine."

He ignored her, and continued to thump everything he passed. The noise of wood thumping wood echoed around the ravine. Would it scare away any animals, or bring them to see what was going on?

"We should find Kerberos and return to the house."

"What do you think it was in the bush?"

"Probably Kerberos again. Think before you throw stones in future, you could have hurt him."

The bushes moved again.

"Henry, stop."

Hope stepped past him, wincing on her weak ankle. Hoping it was just Kerberos looking for his stick, she pushed the bush out of the way.

Kerberos crouched on the other side, sniffing the ground. He raised his nose and stared into the bushes, then began to growl.

"Henry, step back," Hope said, but that just encouraged him to move toward her.

Something large and dark moved between the bushes on the far side of the stream. She couldn't see details in the shadows, but it looked as tall as she was, and stood on two legs. Could it be Pat? No, he must stand at least a foot taller.

But she had barely a second to consider the identity of the prowler before Kerberos barked and raced across the stream, spraying water into the air wherever his paws touched down. The bushes shook as the prowler backed away.

"Kerberos, come back," Hope shouted.

Intent on his prey, he vanished into the bushes. The plants shook as the dog hunted the prowler, with no apparent concern for his own safety.

Henry tried to follow, but Hope grabbed his shoulder and pushed him behind her.

"Kerberos. Come here, boy," she shouted again.

The only movement she could see was the dark shape of the prowler running through the undergrowth further down the stream, now hunched over as though moving on four legs rather than two.

She shouted again. Henry put his fingers between his lips and whistled.

The bushes continued to shake, but Kerberos trotted from them with his tail wagging, and blood on his muzzle. Henry knelt and patted him.

"Good guard dog, Kerberos," Henry said. "You protected both of us."

Hope crouched and examined Kerberos' muzzle. She could see no sign of injury, so the blood must have come from whatever he was fighting. Hopefully a dumb animal, and not a villager who had decided to come and spy on them. Or one of Pat's smugglers making their way inland with their ill-gotten goods, though, in that case, perhaps that might convince them to take those goods elsewhere.

"It was a deer," Henry said.

Hope shook her head. More likely, it was the same thing Pat had disturbed earlier, whatever that might be.

"I do not think that was a deer."

Henry took a few steps in the direction the prowler had run, Kerberos at his heels.

"Henry, come back. We should return to the house."

He ignored her, and continued walking.

"I will get a gun from Father, and, when we see the deer again, I can shoot it."

He strode ahead of her. By the time Hope caught up with him, they had almost reached the end of the ravine. In the half an hour since they had left the area, part of the slope at the side of the ravine had slid down into the stream, and water was pooling beside the pile as it worked to dig a route past the dirt that temporarily blocked its movement.

Henry stared at a dark hole in the slope, perhaps five feet tall and four across, and Kerberos sniffed around it. It wasn't there before, and didn't look like it should be there.

"Can we go in?" Henry said, as Hope opened her mouth to tell him to stay away. That he even asked showed he was as worried as she was by the thought of tunnels beneath the house.

"What is it?" he said.

"Pat said that smugglers dug tunnels from the sea to houses on the coast, so they could bring goods into the country without being caught by the customs men. It is probably an abandoned tunnel that has been buried here for decades."

"Let's explore."

He took a step toward the hole.

If the tunnel collapsed while they were inside, like the hole on the moor the previous day, no-one would ever find them.

"No. We are returning to the house before you get into more trouble. That tunnel could collapse at any moment."

For once, he accepted her instruction, and she kept a good hold on his hand as she hobbled back along the stream. With her ankle injured, she couldn't climb up the steep slope near the tunnel, and the dirt would collapse beneath them if they did.

As they approached the shallow end of the ravine, they found Pat sitting by the stream with his fishing rod. Was he was using the rod as an excuse to look for her? Two fish lying on a blanket alongside him implied that he had been there for some time.

Perhaps they could go back, and try to climb the slope where he couldn't see them? But, before she could move, he turned and looked their way.

"Didn't Mr Hodges say not to come down here, miss?" he said with a smile.

"He did, but Kerberos ran down, and we had to fetch him back."

Pat nodded. "I'm sure that's God's truth, miss."

As he spoke, the fishing line jerked, and he pulled it from the water. Another fish hung from the hook, its body twisting and shaking as it tried to escape. Pat pulled it toward him, and held it in his hand as he twisted the hook from its mouth.

"I thought Father told you to go back to the house to repair the drain-pipe?" Hope said.

"Ah, miss, from the look of the rust, it's been up there for years. I reckon it can survive a while longer without me risking me neck climbing up there."

She led Henry past, still limping on her twisted ankle.

"What happened to you, miss?" Pat said.

"I hurt my ankle coming down the slope."

Pat stood. "Here, I can carry you back to the house."

She was almost ready to accept his offer if it would eliminate the pain. But not quite.

"I will make my own way, thank you."

"Where have you been?" William said as they entered the lounge. "Mrs Phillips is cooking Henry's bird for dinner, and then I thought you could sing while I play the piano."

Then he saw Hope hobbling on her twisted ankle. "What have you done?"

"Henry was throwing sticks for Kerberos, and we lost track of time. Then I fell, and twisted my ankle."

She slumped down in one of Howard's armchairs, glad to rest and take the weight off the ankle for a moment. The pain faded to a dull ache as she lifted it off the ground.

"Henry," William said. "Go and ask Mrs Phillips when our dinner will be ready."

He waited for Henry to leave the room before speaking again.

"You should not encourage Henry in such antics."

"I did not. He went into the ravine despite my attempts to stop him. He will not listen to anyone, certainly not me."

"Have you seen Pat?"

"I was just talking to him down by the stream. He is fishing for supper."

William leaned closer and spoke quietly. "You are not to spend any more time with him. I will not see you make fools of us again."

"There is nothing between Pat and myself."

"You and I both know that is not true. If we did not need the help, I would have dismissed him already."

She nodded, unsure of whether she wanted Pat to leave or stay. William was right that he wasn't a proper suitor, and she had no idea whether he really felt anything for her, or whether she should feel anything for him. She just wanted to be back home in London, where life was much simpler, and Herbert could take her away from all the family's problems.

"Go and see Mrs Phillips," William said. "She may be able to do something for your ankle."

Hope hobbled to the kitchen. Mrs Phillips looked up as Hope took the steps one at a time, wincing as each step sent a sharp pain up her leg.

"Put that up and rest, miss," she said.

Hope sat on a chair, and rested her ankle on another. Mrs Phillips cooked up a poultice, then smeared it over her ankle. It stank like rotten cabbage, so Hope hoped it would at least do some good, to compensate for the smell.

Marbles clunked together under the table.

"Henry," Hope said, "I thought Father wanted you to return to tell us when dinner would be ready."

The marbles continued clunking as he played.

"Still be a little while," Mrs Phillips said. She looked at Hope with dark bags showing under her eyes.

"Are you unwell?" Hope said.

"It's all right, miss. I just didn't sleep much last night."

"The storms?"

"I've had such funny dreams since we arrived here. I don't like living in such a strange place."

"What kind of dreams."

"Oh, miss, I really don't like to say."

The kitchen door opened, and Pat strode down the steps with a pile of fish wrapped in the blanket. He slapped them down on the table with a wet thud.

"There you are, Mrs Phillips."

Mrs Phillips unwrapped the fish as Pat smirked and winked at Hope. She lowered her eyes as her heart thumped in her chest.

"That'll keep us going for a day or two," Mrs Phillips said. "I'll bake a nice fish pie."

Pat picked up a mug and walked to the beer keg. "I reckon I deserve a good drink for that."

Henry's head poked out from under the table. "Can I have some?"

Hope would never hear the end of it from her father if she allowed him to start drinking. "No, Henry."

He frowned. Pat nodded toward her. "I'll get you some when your sister is gone."

"I should be going anyway. I hope Mrs Phillips can keep you two out of trouble."

"Oh, miss," Mrs Phillips said. "You shouldn't walk on that ankle until the poultice has done its work."

Pat pulled back a chair, sat and put his feet up on the table. "I doubt you have anything more important to do, eh miss?"

She looked at him, and he stared back, eyes focused like a hunter sure he has caught his prey. Blood rushed to her cheeks. Perhaps she was already caught. The man was a rogue, but life with him would be far more interesting than the men her father had introduced her to in London. More so even than Herbert.

"I could be reading the Bible, as Father told me to."

"I reckon you read that more than enough. It always seemed boring to me, except the fighting and begatting."

A heathen too. "I do not think that Father wanted me to spend much time on those parts."

"You should, miss. Won't be long now, before you have a husband begatting with you."

She opened her mouth to speak, but Pat laughed and turned away. "Mrs Phillips, why are young ladies like arrows?"

"Because they go all aquiver around their beau," Mrs Phillips said. "Why don't you finish your drink, then find something useful to do?"

"I am doing something useful. I'm clearing out the old beer before it goes off. I wouldn't want the old man to come back and find his drink had gone to waste."

"Idle hands do the Devil's work. I'm sure Mr Hodges can find something to keep them busy."

Pat emptied his mug and winked at Hope. "I'll see you later, miss."

Somehow, she already knew he would.

CHAPTER NINE

That evening, through dinner, then her father's piano playing, then prayers for Uncle Howard, Hope thought more and more about the hole in the ravine. If it was really a smugglers' tunnel, it might provide some clues about Howard's peculiar artifacts in the cellar. If he had found one of their tunnels, perhaps he had found his artifacts in those tunnels. She had to return to it, and investigate the depths for herself.

"Leviticus 22:21," William said, bringing her back to the present from her daydreams of exploring below the house.

"And the men of her city shall stone her with stones that she die," she said, feeling her cheeks blushing. "Because she hath wrought folly, playing the whore in her father's house: so shalt thou put evil away from among you."

Was this another accusation about her and Pat? His cheeks seemed as red as hers.

"What is a whore?" Henry said.

"That is Deuteronomy 22:21," William said.

"Mother, what is a whore?" Henry said again.

William coughed. "It is a girl who does not do as her father tells her."

Hope laughed, as he seemed even more embarrassed by the mistake than she was. She had always confused Deuteronomy and Leviticus, and now she remembered the correct verse.

"And whosoever offereth a sacrifice of peace offerings unto the Lord in beeves or sheep, it shall be accepted."

"Good, good," William said. "But you can do better. Study until you know all the words, not just the few you choose to remember."

"I see Howard in the garden," Eliza said.

Hope's heart skipped a beat as Eliza raised her arm, and pointed her finger at the window.

"William, bring Howard to me. We must talk."

They looked where she pointed. The light was dim outside as the sun sank toward the horizon, and a few rain drops had splattered across the glass. Nothing moved in the garden, other than leaves blowing in the wind.

"My dear," William said, "I am afraid you are imagining things."

"He was there, watching me, only a moment ago."

William glanced at Hope and sighed. "Come, Eliza. I think you should lie down."

He took Eliza's hand and led her from the room.

"Bring Howard to see me," Eliza said.

"I will stay with you for a while," William said. "Perhaps he will come to see us both."

"I want to go for a walk," Henry said.

"Come on," Hope said.

She had to return to the tunnel, or she would be tossing and turning all night, wondering what was down there. But what if she ran into the prowler again, and in the dark?

Hopefully Kerberos had convinced it to give the place a wide berth, as she wouldn't be able to run again until her ankle recovered. The sun was setting, but, if she took a lantern, it might scare away any animal which lived in the area. In case that wouldn't be enough, she could take Kerberos with her.

However, he had his own ideas. They found him warming himself by a bonfire in the garden. He looked up, but showed no indication of wanting to join them. Pat stood nearby, his shirt off, an axe in his hand and sweat on his body. He was chopping wooden boards and burning them.

"Evening, miss."

"What are you doing?"

Pat picked up another board, chopped it into pieces on a log, and threw it onto the fire. "Cleaning up some of the mess your uncle left. There's not much use for the broken boards I pulled from the windows, when we have so much coal."

Henry strolled toward the fire. "Can I help?"

Pat looked at Hope. If Henry swung an axe, he was sure to chop off his own arms. But he could manage to throw wood on the fire. She nodded.

"Come here," Pat said.

Henry hurried to him, and Pat handed him chunks of chopped wood. Henry walked to the fire and began throwing them into the flames.

"Do not get too close," Hope said. "I do not want you to see you get burned."

Pat smashed up another board with his axe. "You look after him more than your mother does."

"Mother is sick. Father hoped that coming here might help her recover, but so far we have been disappointed."

Pat handed more wood to Henry, who seemed content to run back and forth carrying it, and throw it onto the fire.

"How's your ankle?"

"I can walk, but it still pains me when I put weight on it."

Pat nodded. He lifted one of the planks and chopped much of the wood away, then smoothed the rest, shaving the edges with the axe blade. He handed it to her. "Lean on that, if it hurts too much."

She held it and leaned on it as she took a step onto her wounded foot. The wood was hardly up to the standards of Howard's walking sticks in the study, but it reduced the weight on the ankle, and eased the pain.

"Thank you. That will certainly help."

Henry threw wood on the fire and laughed as it burned, the flames growing higher the more wood he threw. Kerberos rolled over, exposing his belly to the heat.

"William says Hope is a whore," Henry said.

Pat stared at her, wide-eyed. She shook her head.

"Henry, he did not say that."

"He said girls who disobey their fathers are whores."

She looked at Pat. "We were discussing Deuteronomy."

He nodded and smirked. "There are a lot of whores in the Bible, miss. If God hadn't written it, the preachers wouldn't let anyone read it."

He chopped up more wood and handed some to Henry, who raced toward the fire with his arms full.

"Be careful, Henry," Hope said. "You don't want to hurt your ankle too."

"Are you enjoying your time here?" Pat said.

"Father says I should not talk to you. He is afraid that you harbour dishonourable thoughts about me, while I am sure that you do."

"I might well, miss."

"Apparently I may go native and become a Catholic fishwife if I spend time with you. He said that if he did not need you to help around the house, he would have dismissed you by now, to protect my virtue."

"If he didn't need my help, there'd be no point paying me to sit around doing nothing, miss. Not that I'd mind that, your uncle still has beer I haven't had time to drink."

"Either way, he does not seem happy with you tonight."

Pat sniggered. "He wanted another game of croquet, but the balls have disappeared. He reckons I hid them for a joke."

"And did you?"

"Who do you think I am, miss? I put them away after the last game, and now they're gone, I don't know where they are."

Henry tugged on Hope's arm. "I want to go back now."

"You can go if you want. I think Pat is running out of work for you."

Henry looked toward the house. "I do not want to walk by myself."

"I should get back to work," Pat said. "Mr Hodges wants me to take more coal in for Mrs Phillips when I'm done here. At this rate she won't have room to move in the kitchen soon."

She led Henry back to the house. Their parents argued in their room upstairs, though the window muffled their words. The sun had set, but she still wanted to see the tunnel that day.

After taking Henry to his bedroom, she took a lantern to find her way, and walked along the edge of the ravine, slowed by the need to resort to Pat's stick when her ankle became too painful. No more of the slope had collapsed, and she listened for any sign of movement as she limped along the edge. Walking along the stream would be difficult in the dark, and just invite the prowler to come prowling. She would have felt happier if Kerberos had joined her, but, the last time she saw him, he was still enjoying the fading heat of Pat's fire.

When she neared the hole, she was able to scramble down the slope by supporting herself with the stick and trunks of nearby trees. The loose soil slid beneath her feet, and she would have a long walk along the stream if she couldn't climb back up afterwards.

She stepped cautiously toward the hole, and looked inside. The lantern's glow illuminated a rough tunnel leading steeply downward, pointing vaguely toward the house. Even if she managed to climb down, it was too steep to climb back up without a rope to assist her. The hole's interior was too dark to see far, but there were recent scrapes and gouges in the dirt outside, as though an animal had crawled in or out.

She stepped to the edge of the drop, and listened for any sound from below. But all she could hear was the wind shaking leaves along the ravine, and the waves breaking on the rocks below. She picked up a stone and dropped it, so it tumbled into the darkness. It rattled against the tunnel walls as it fell.

A faint moaning sound rose from below, like the sound she had heard in the cellar. Had she run into a gang of smugglers? If so, they would probably not appreciate her presence there.

A twig snapped behind her, and she turned. The prowler was following her again. She raised the lantern as the bushes shook. She should have brought something to protect herself. She picked it up a large stone from the ground, and raised it ready to hit them. If that failed, she had the walking stick.

The bushes moved apart, grasped by large hands. A light brown face peered out between them, eyes shining in the light from the lantern.

"Evening, miss," Pat said.

Hope lowered the stone. "What are you doing here? You scared me half senseless."

He smiled. "I saw you coming down here against your father's wishes, and I thought I should make sure no harm came to you. You need a man to protect you, miss. You don't know what could be down here."

He stepped out of the bushes toward her.

"I think I know who I need protection from," Hope said.

He stepped closer. She could smell the beer on his breath and the sweat on his body. She should have been disgusted, but wanted him to come closer so she could smell more.

"Really, miss? Who would that be?"

"I am sure you are glad to see that I am not in any need of protection. I wished to see what the landslide had dislodged here, and ensure it would not affect the garden."

He turned his head to look past her, now apparently more interested in the tunnel than her presence. "I don't remember seeing this before."

She stepped away from him, and held the lantern close to the entrance. "Could it be your smugglers' tunnel?"

He stood behind her, looking over her shoulder into the darkness. His breath warmed her neck, and blew her hair.

"I don't see why they would be coming up here."

She turned to him. "Maybe it goes down to the beach?"

"I don't feel like climbing down to find out. Do you?"

No. Something which shouldn't be in the estate had made the tunnel. Human or animal, she could only hope that it had gone.

"Not tonight," Hope said.

"You know, your father questioned me about those flowers, when I was taking the coal in."

"I am sorry. I should not have told him, but he saw them as I was taking them from my room."

Pat sniggered. "Nothing to apologize for, miss. I told him I hadn't given them to you and you must just be making fun with him. That seemed to satisfy him for now. I think he trusts you less than he trusts me."

"I am sorry you had to lie."

"I don't feel bad about lying, because the flowers I gave you didn't look like the ones your father was carrying."

"I do not know what happened to them. I left them by my bed, and in the morning they were shrivelled and dead. Could the water have killed them?"

Pat shrugged. "It hasn't harmed anyone at the village, but perhaps we should boil it before anyone drinks it here."

Should she tell him any more about their explorations? No, but, she had to know what was hidden in the cellar.

"We went into the cellar. Uncle Howard has many strange things down there, and there is a locked door at the far end. I would like to know what is behind the door."

"Maybe we should take a look, miss. Of course I would have to come to protect you."

"Father locked the cellar again and has the keys. And none of those keys would open the locked door, we tried them all."

"I know a few things about locks. Perhaps I can open it."

"Can you do that? The cellar door has several locks and the keys are a peculiar design."

Pat nodded. "Perhaps not, then. We could try the cellar windows, but, even if one opens, I wouldn't fit between the bars." His gaze roamed from the ground, up her body to her face. "You might."

He held out his hand to her.

"And what is that for?" Hope said.

"You're not going to climb out of here on your own, miss."

As they strolled back to the house, Hope glanced at the well. Before, it had seemed just another inconspicuous piece of daily life, but could it really put their lives in danger? If it killed the plants overnight, what could it be doing to them?

"We should look at the well, since we are passing."

"Could be a dead animal in there."

Hope shivered. "Or Uncle Howard? Perhaps he fell while fetching water?"

Pat's habitual smirk vanished from his face. "I'll get us a rope."

He found one in the stable, and they tied the lantern to the end, then lowered it into the well. It twisted and swung as it descended toward the water, its glow illuminating a few feet around it. The stone walls were breaking up, and the gaps between stones were filled with moss, but they saw no sign of dead animals, dead uncles or strange plants in the water.

"What are you doing?"

Pat and Hope jumped at the sound, and released the rope. The lantern splashed down in the water and went out. William carried a lantern of his own, and held it up in front of their faces. The smell of Howard's wine was on his breath, blowing toward them as he spoke.

"We were looking down in the well," Hope said, after she had recovered her wits, "in case the water that killed the plants might be poisonous to us."

William glanced at Pat, then at the rope leading into the well. "And you felt you must do this late at night? By yourselves? Without even consulting me?"

"Sorry, sir," Pat said. "We should have waited 'til morning and brought you with us. But Miss Hope felt that it was too important."

"It is my fault. I asked Pat to assist me. I was worried that someone could become ill from the water, and did not want to have to wait a moment longer to investigate."

"I'll be going, sir," Pat said. "I think you can help Miss Hope yourself."

"Pat, collect some more coal from the pile and take it to Mrs Phillips. She never seems to have enough."

Pat nodded, and walked toward the rear of the house.

William leaned over the side of the well and looked down, then pulled on the rope. "What is this?"

"We lowered a lantern into the well, so we could see what was down there. You surprised us when you called out, and we dropped it."

"If the water was clean before, it will not be with oil and glass down there."

"I am sorry, Father. I meant well. Pat felt that we should not drink the water again unless it is boiled."

William studied her face. Did he believe she was telling the truth? Of course not. But how could she tell him about the trip to the tunnel? Would that be better than any sins he imagined, or worse?

He nodded. "That could well be worthwhile. I will tell Mrs Phillips. Now let us pull up the lantern and go to bed."

They pulled the rope from the well. The glass of the lantern was still intact, and only a little oil had leaked. They carried it back to the house.

William looked at the stick. "What is that?"

"Pat made it for me. To help me walk easily, until my ankle improves."

"Not walking on it would be better."

"Uncle Howard has several walking sticks in his study. Those would work better."

"You are not entering the study. And you are to leave Howard's property alone."

He stopped to look at the sky, then at his watch. "It is strange, the sun should not have set so soon at this time of year."

"I had not thought of it. The sun just does what it does."

"The sun follows rules of celestial mechanics. It cannot just move on its own."

"Perhaps the sun no longer wants to obey the rules we have imposed on it. Perhaps it wishes to be free of the rules, to act however it likes."

"The sun will do what the laws of science tell us it must do."

"Clearly it will not."

William stared at her, then turned away, and they walked back to the house in silence. He escorted Hope to her bedroom.

As he closed the door, she sat on the bed and opened her journal to begin bringing it up to date before she looked for Pat. Then a key clattered in the lock.

She hobbled to the door and turned the handle, but the door remained shut. "What are you doing?"

"I do not want you leaving your room again tonight. If I find you alone with that man another time, I will confine you to your room whenever you are not with me."

She banged her hand on the door. "Let me out. I am not a little girl to be locked in my room for misbehaving."

"That is precisely what you are. Perhaps, in the morning, you will have learned your lesson. Besides, a good rest will do wonders for your ankle."

"Father!" she called, and continued to bang on the door. But she could hear his feet tapping on the stairs as he returned to his room.

CHAPTER TEN

Hope sat on the bed again. What more could she do? She could hardly bash down the door, and the window was too high to climb from.

As she filled out the day's entry in her journal, she heard footsteps on the stairs, then clicking at the door. Perhaps her father had decided to return and apologize for his behaviour? The wine couldn't have done him any good.

Then the lock clicked, and the door swung open. In the dim light of her candles, Pat's face peered around the edge. He held up the key-ring with the strange cellar keys.

"How did you get that?" she whispered.

"I picked the lock to your dad's room while he was up here with you. From what you said, I must have found the keys to the cellar."

Hope closed the journal and slid her feet into her slippers. "Then let us go before he discovers they are gone."

Pat unlocked the cellar door and swung it open. Hope peered into the familiar darkness. Should she be more scared of what might be hidden deep in the cellar, or what her father would do if he discovered they had been down there? Pat carried a metal bar, to open the far door if the keys failed.

Nothing in the cellar appeared to have been disturbed in the time since Hope had been there with the others. If smugglers had crawled into it from their tunnels, they were very tidy smugglers.

When they reached the far door, Pat examined the lock and tried all the keys in turn. They fit, but none would turn.

"Can you break it?" Hope said.

He pushed a bent piece of metal into the lock. "I'd sooner open the lock."

Hope held the lantern as he twisted the lock-pick. They stood in the narrow pool of light the lantern cast, surrounded by seemingly endless darkness. As the metal clicked and scraped in the lock, she listened for any sound of intruders.

Or her father.

Pat finally pulled the lock-pick out. "Not going to work that way."

He picked up the metal bar and pushed one end into the gap between the door and the frame. He heaved on it and heaved again, until the lock broke away from the frame, and the door swung away from them. He took the lantern, and peered around the edge of the door, then pushed it wide open.

Behind the door was a room with rough stone walls coated with black dust. Perhaps a coal cellar when the house was first built? Howard must have cleared it out and added the door for his own peculiar use.

Pat shone the lantern around. A waist-high flat rock stood in the centre of the room, with manacles on chains screwed into the rock, and piles of jars on shelves around those walls. They stepped inside, and he placed the lantern on the rock so they could both see.

Scattered on the ground were smaller chunks of the black stone. Hope picked up a few and placed them on the rock. Two fit together as though part of some more complex shape. At the furthest end of the alcove, markings were scratched in the wall. Even in the dim light, they were no language Hope had ever seen in London, but intertwined curved shapes like those on Howard's books.

Dark brown smears coated the rock itself, and Pat ran his fingers across one.

"I pray that is not Uncle Howard's blood," Hope said.

Pat raised his fingers and rubbed them together. "Whatever it was, it's dry now."

With some trepidation, Hope lifted a jar from the shelf and placed it on the rock, then lifted the lid. She leaned closer, and coughed as the stench of the thick yellow preservative inside burned her lungs. She wafted it away from her face, then took another look.

A gnarled, scaly grey-skinned hand with thin fingers and long claws floated in the liquid, roughly severed at the wrist as though hacked off with a sword. Not Uncle Howard's, but it reminded her of the hands of the creature in her dream. Could her memory be playing tricks on her? She might believe that, if she hadn't written the dream in her journal.

She placed the jar on the rock, as Pat examined the wall markings.

"Take a look at this," she said.

Pat peered in. "What in God's name is that?"

He reached into the jar to pull out the hand, but Hope stopped him.

"I do not think that God has anything to do with it. I would not risk touching it, who knows what kind of creature it might have come from?"

Pat took another jar from the shelf and lifted the lid. Hope stepped over to look in, but he lifted it away from her.

"I don't think you want to see this, miss."

"Nonsense." Had he found part of Uncle Howard?

"I'm sure, miss."

"I want to see."

He placed the jar on the rock, the lid alongside it. She raised the lantern and looked in.

It contained a grey-skinned, scaly penis, perhaps six inches long. She stared at it for a moment, blushing but curious, before she closed the lid.

"I hope that is not Uncle Howard's."

"I don't think we should be looking any further down here, miss."

She had expected to be more disconcerted by Pat than by their findings, but the reality seemed to be the opposite. The strange room had distracted him from his games. Her heart didn't want to know what was in the other jars, but her head couldn't resist opening the next.

"Let us examine another," she said, and carried it to the rock. She lifted the lid.

Inside floated a grey cabbage-like mass.

"What is that?" she said.

"That's a brain, miss. Bigger than any animal's I ever saw."

She slammed the lid on the jar.

"Perhaps you are right," she said, and backed away.

Her foot hit something on the floor. A notebook lay by her foot. She picked it up and opened it.

Water had damaged some pages, but the notebook was filled with diagrams of the house and caves, and writing in the same characters as those on the wall. Perhaps the smugglers used some special kind of map, and language, so others couldn't read their directions?

She handed it to Pat as he approached. He flipped through the diagrams, then dropped it on the rock.

"Let's go," he said. "I think we've seen enough."

He picked up the lantern, put his hand on her arm and led her away, then pulled the door closed behind them. It would never lock again, but it wouldn't obviously appear broken to a casual glance from a distance.

Hope had expected to feel better when she knew what was behind the locked door, but she would be no happier alone in her bed at night knowing those things were below her feet but not what they were or why they were there. Had Uncle Howard robbed graveyards to satisfy some perverse curiosity he had developed during the war? Her father wouldn't want that to become common knowledge, and besmirch her mother's family name. Perhaps Howard had told her mother of such a taste, and caused her nervous condition.

"The hand looked like no man or woman I have ever seen," she said. "But the other parts..."

"Let's not speak about this again. I don't want to know what your uncle has been doing down here. I can almost believe the stories about him now."

"I am sure that was blood on the rock. What if that really is Uncle Howard in those jars?"

"Then it will be best for everyone that none but us two ever knows."

"We should take the notebook. There could be something of value in it. The maps show tunnels around the house."

Pat led her away from the door, placed the lantern on a shelf, and turned to her. He leaned forward and lowered his face to kiss her on her cheek. Her body shook at his unexpected–not to say unwanted–touch.

"Do not do that again. If my father finds out he will dismiss you."

"Then your father will find it's a long walk up the cliffs back to Graiguengal without the horses."

He put his arms around her back, and pulled her to him. He kissed her again, this time on the lips, an experience she never had before, even with Herbert. The taste of stale beer filled her mouth as his tongue explored inside it. He slid his hand down her back and squeezed her ass as he held his body against hers.

When he was done, he released her. Then she recovered her senses, and slapped him.

"Do not ever take advantage of your position. I will tell my father."

He smiled at her. "No, miss, you will not."

He was right. She should report his actions to her father, but it would only cause more trouble for them all. And, as little as she wanted to admit it, his behaviour wasn't entirely unpleasant. With her mother in her condition, family life had become so complicated and uncomfortable, whereas Pat's attitude to life seemed anything but complicated. He did as he pleased, and cared little for the consequences. Oh, what she would give for a life as simple as his.

Yet no-one could come to her assistance if he wanted to overpower her. He could have his way with her in the dark of the cellar, then disappear into the nearby villages where he would never be found. They wouldn't hand over one of their own to outsiders from London.

Worse, as her heart fluttered at his touch, she wasn't sure she would even try to stop him.

"And if you do tell him," Pat added, "he might wonder what you were doing down here, a place where he forbade you to go. With a man he forbade you to be alone with. When you were supposed to be locked in your room."

"He might think that you came here intentionally to be with me and then made up a story to excuse yourself. I might even believe that myself."

"I did not come here to be with you."

He pushed her back against the wall, so the cold stones pressed against her back while his warm body pressed against her chest.

"I know you don't like this house any more than I do. Come away with me. We can ride to the village tonight and onwards tomorrow. Your parents will never find us."

For a second, she imagined herself riding away with the man, living with him in one of the cottages she had seen by the side of the road on their journey. Then she imagined herself a few years from now, one of the plump, wrinkled women with a gaggle of children following her around as she washed their laundry and hung it from a rough line outside the house. That fate didn't appeal any more than her current life.

"I will not go away with you," she said.

"Never?"

"No, and do not ask me again," she said, because if he did ask her again, she knew she would damn the consequences and say yes.

He stepped back and picked up the lantern. "I will escort you to your bedroom then, miss. And we should return the keys to Mr Hodges before he realizes they are missing."

"I can make my own way," she said.

As another storm thundered outside the house, Pat followed her every step back to her door, then locked it, so her father wouldn't realize that she had left the room.

It was only while she lay in bed writing about the evening's events in her journal that she realized that, in the excitement of Pat's attentions, she forgot to pick up the notebook.

CHAPTER ELEVEN

The orange sun hung low in the sky as Hope found herself trotting through the undergrowth in the ravine, on all fours like the prowler. Had her experience with it provoked the dream? Her body had the same clawed hands that they had found in the cellar and seen in her earlier dream, but that didn't disturb her. She didn't look to see whether she had any of the other body parts from Howard's jars.

She was chasing something through the ravine. She stopped to hide behind a tree, and sniffed the air for the scent of her prey. Bushes moved to her right and she crouched low. The scent came from that direction, and she crept toward it, trying not to make a sound that would warn the prey. The bushes continued to move ahead of her.

She sniffed the scent and pushed the leaves apart, then poked her head through the gap.

Henry was swimming in the pool, looking away from her. His clothes lay on the ground beside it, where they had sat when they swam there before.

She screeched, then pushed herself through the bush and raced toward him. He turned toward the noise, and his eyes widened and mouth opened at the sight of her approach. Then, as she plunged into the water, he turned away and swam to the far side.

She chased him, somehow able to swim in this body, even though unable in her own. He climbed out of the pool, and ran down the ravine toward the sea. She swam to the edge of the pool, then pulled herself out, her claws digging into the mud. She screeched again, before chasing after him.

Her breath hardly accelerated as her muscular arms and legs pounded on the ground and propelled her toward him with ease. He dodged between two trees. She raced around them, so she didn't need to slow down.

Henry was running fast, and she could hear his panting breath ahead. He looked back over his shoulder, and his eyes widened as he saw she was gaining on him.

He ran on, smashing through the bushes, and dodging from side to side to avoid the trees. She was getting closer, his legs only a few feet in front of her claws, and he couldn't escape. He must have realized that too, because he dodged behind a tree trunk and grabbed a branch which was hanging loose.

She was about to jump at him, when he broke the branch from the tree and spun toward her. Instead, she turned and slid to a stop, her claws scrabbling for grip as her speed threatened to send her flying past him.

As she crept toward Henry, he swung the branch at her, but she dodged the blow. He swung again, but she lowered her head and the branch passed above her, the leaves brushing her back and the twigs scraping against her tough skin. She smelled the fear on him and the sweat of the chase. Saliva built up in her throat, and she screeched again.

She lunged for him, but misjudged the attack. Henry swung the branch and it smashed into her side. She landed on her hands and feet, turned back toward him and snapped her teeth together, eager for his blood.

Henry swung the branch toward her again, but she dodged it to snap at his wrist, and felt her teeth draw blood. He pulled the wounded arm back and swung the branch with his good arm. It hit her on the side, but with little force. She yelped, but continued her attack.

She sprung up, mouth opened wide, reaching for his throat.

Hope awoke, gasping. She had lain awake until the early hours listening to the thunder and thinking of her experiences that night, both those with Pat and those in Howard's secret room. Then she struggled with nightmares, of which that was the last. It had seemed so real at the time, and her behaviour so natural, that it disturbed her far more than the others.

Her body ached and wanted to rest for the remainder of the morning, but, if she slept again, the dreams might grow even worse. She opened her Bible and began to read, hoping that would pass some time in a profitable manner. But then she heard Pat's voice outside the house, and couldn't concentrate on reading while he was talking.

She walked to the window and pulled open the curtain. He was speaking to her father in the garden. Their voices were loud, but distant enough that she couldn't make out their words. Pat's face turned toward the window and his eyes met hers. She pulled herself back and closed the curtain, heart pounding.

Soon afterwards, a key clattered in the lock. Mrs Phillips pushed the door open, then walked to Hope's bed carrying her breakfast on a tray.

"Mr Hodges says you can come out now, miss," she said, then placed the tray on the bed.

"I think I would prefer to stay here awhile,"

"You can't mope in here forever, miss," she said and walked out, leaving the door unlocked.

Hope ate the breakfast, then spent most of the morning reading. Her head told her to stay as far from Pat as she could, but her heart wanted to rush down and see him again. Her head won, for now. She had to convince her father that she wouldn't cause trouble if she wanted her freedom.

Her mother came to her room late in the morning.

"Go to Mrs Phillips and bring me more medicine," she said. "I am feeling unwell."

Was that a sign her mother had been upset by the journey and Howard's disappearance, and time was now healing her?

Hope's ankle took her weight with only an occasional twinge after the night's rest, and she went downstairs. A pool of light shone on the carpet at the bottom. The study door was open, letting sunlight in.

She looked in, expecting to see her father. But it was empty. She looked down the hallway and listened, but could neither see nor hear any sign of him.

She stepped into the study to the sound of the ticking clocks. Although they had reset them only a few days before, they all now showed different times.

The doors of the bookcases were still locked, and her father had the key. She should have thought to have Pat open it for her while he had the keys. She sat in front of the desk instead, and pulled on the drawer handles. They, at least, were unlocked and opened without problem.

She pulled papers from the drawers and sifted through them. Most were written in the same language they had seen down in the cellar, but one in particular caught her attention.

On the paper were two sketches, roughly drawn, as though they were made in a hurry. One showed the same machines and conical creatures that she had seen in her earlier dream. She would almost believe she had imagined the similarity, if she hadn't noted those very details in her journal. What could that mean? Had she glimpsed a similar picture in Howard's books when she was first in this study, and made that part of her dream? Or had he dreamed the same dream?

The other showed the house itself surrounded by more of the strange machines, with spider-like creatures crawling over them, and large black birds in the sky. Where could Uncle Howard have received that vision from?

Should she keep the pictures, or return them to their rightful place? If she took them, it would be a perpetual reminder that something very strange had happened in the house. If only the whole trip was a dream, and she could wake in the morning to find herself in her own bed in London. That surprise, she wouldn't mind.

"What are you doing in here?"

She closed the drawer as she heard her father's voice behind her. "I was looking for you, Father."

"What for?"

"I just wanted to know what you were doing today."

He unlocked the gun cabinet and removed the shotguns. "I will try to find a deer so we can have venison for dinner."

"Be careful," she said, as she thought back to her strange dreams of creatures hunting in the ravine. Dream or not, she still felt she should treat it as a warning.

William stared at her, seemingly unable to decide how to reply.

"I will," he said, after a moment. "Go and see Mrs Phillips while I am outside. She must have something useful you can do."

"Why have the clocks lost time?" Hope said.

William checked the shotgun. "The times they show have been different every day. I think they must be broken. Perhaps Howard kept them here for his amusement."

He led her toward the door into the hallway. She stepped through it and he closed and locked it behind them.

When she returned to the kitchen, Mrs Phillips was piercing seeds with a needle, and placing them in a bowl by the fire as Henry sat watching her.

"What are you doing?" Hope said.

Mrs Phillips looked up from the seeds for a moment.

"Making Mother's medicine," Henry said.

"Where is Pat?"

Mrs Phillips looked sheepish. "Did Mr Hodges not tell you?"

Hope shook her head. Mrs Phillips leaned closer to her.

"He dismissed Pat this morning," she whispered. "You should have heard the shouting. I don't know what it was about, but Mr Hodges seemed about fit to kill him."

Dismissed? Just when her life was changing for the better, her father made it worse. She had to find Pat, wherever he might have gone.

"Where is he now?"

"Mr Hodges is upstairs somewhere, miss."

"I meant Pat."

"I don't know miss. Must have left three hours ago. He sure wasn't happy, he'll be half-way back to that Graiguengal by now."

Hope stared at her. The world was spinning, and blood rushing through her ears. She put her hand on the table to steady herself.

"You are sure he left?"

"I saw with my own eyes Mr Hodges take him to the gate, then he walked off down the track without looking back," Mrs Phillips said. She patted Hope's hand. "It's all for the best, miss. You shouldn't be getting involved with a man like that, they'll promise you everything, then leave you nothing but a baby with no father."

Hope sat, her legs unable to hold her weight.

"I have just become so used to having him around. I cannot imagine spending the rest of the summer alone."

"You have your family, miss."

But she felt more alone there with her family than by herself in a crowded London street.

"We can go exploring again," Henry said.

"And I'm always down here if you need a chat," Mrs Phillips added.

Hope nodded. Sad to say, she felt closer to their housekeeper than her own parents.

"Here," Mrs Phillips said, "I have something for you."

She reached down and hunted through her knitting bag, then pulled out two masses of coloured wool and held one out to each of them. Henry took his and slid it on his head with a smile, a red and blue woollen hat. Hope's was a scarf.

"Thank you," she said, "but I expect they will be more useful in winter than summer."

"I don't know, miss," Mrs Phillips said. "It's getting awfully chilly outside, almost like winter is coming early this year. Or perhaps it's just the wind off the sea."

"We can go back to the ravine," Henry said. "My hat will keep me warm."

"No," Hope said. Even if the ravine had stopped collapsing, she didn't want him to run into the prowler again after her dream. "We should stay out of there as Father told us."

"Those cliffs aren't safe," Mrs Phillips said. "You'll have one heck of a fall if you keep going down there."

"Besides, you should not be in the kitchen, because Father would not want you here."

"But I am helping Mrs Phillips," Henry said.

"He's all right, miss," Mrs Phillips said. "He's not getting in my way. It's nice having a bit of company now Pat is gone."

Henry must be as bored as Hope was of sitting around the house waiting for Uncle Howard to return, and looking for something to entertain himself.

"Be sure you don't make trouble," Hope said.

She strode to the garden to find her father and confront him. She would see Pat again, even if she had to walk all the way to the village herself. Her heart pounded as she thought of what had happened the day before, and what might happen the next time she saw him.

CHAPTER TWELVE

Hope found no sign of her father in the garden, and walked to the gate. Would she see Pat waiting for her in the distance? If she did, she would run to him without even taking the time to return for any of her belongings.

But the gates were locked. She stared through the wide gaps between the bars, but could see only the rough track along the cliff tops. Mrs Phillips was right, Pat had never felt anything for her, and would use his talents to have some village girl in his arms that night. What a fool she had been.

She turned away from the gates. Henry was watching her, wearing his new hat.

"Why are you crying?" he said.

She hadn't even realized she was, but, at his comment, she wiped a tear from her eyes.

"Can we play a game?" he said.

"I do not feel like it. I am going to my room."

She turned to leave, but Henry followed.

"I want to play hide and seek."

She looked down at him. He fidgeted and smiled, eager for something to do, and she couldn't spend the rest of the summer moping over Pat.

"All right. But I think you will be much better able to hide than I can."

She took his hand and led the way past the house, into the garden.

"You can hide first," Hope said. She could safely take her time in finding him, and wouldn't have to rush around, looking for a hiding place herself.

He stood under one of the apple trees. "No, you go. I will count to one hundred," he said, then turned toward the tree, covered his eyes and began to count. As Hope walked toward the wood, he stopped twice as he lost count or skipped some numbers. Whether he counted more or less than the promised hundred, the sooner she found a place to hide, the better.

She strode into the wood, surrounded by trees and bushes. None were particularly large, thanks to the ocean weather, and none looking to be a better hiding place than any other. She walked on, listening for Henry to finish counting over the faint sound of waves breaking on the shore, so she could just pick the nearest tree to hide behind at that point. Even the birds they saw earlier had vanished, as though they had scared them away. Perhaps Henry's attempts at shooting had finally achieved something.

"Coming, ready or not." Henry's words floated through the wood toward her.

A large bush pressed against a thick tree trunk, covering most of one side with a canopy of leaves. Hope pushed the bush far enough from the trunk to create a space she could fit into beneath them. She adjusted her dress, pulling out the cloth until she could sit with discomfort on the twisted trunk, then released the bush, so it moved back. With the leaves in place, she could see out between them without being immediately obvious to anyone looking for her.

The weather was cold for summer, particularly in the shade, and colder still with the damp wood and moss of the trunk pressing against her back. She should have worn her new scarf. Could she hide there long enough to satisfy her hider's honour without lasting long enough to freeze? She wrapped her arms around herself for warmth. If Henry didn't find her quickly, she would 'accidentally' allow him to do so.

Feet crunched over the loose twigs on the ground, and, at the noise, she pushed herself further back into her hiding place, holding her breath as the footsteps approached. Henry walked past and looked from side to side into the trees, but he didn't look back toward where she sat. He continued onward, deeper into the wood, his red hat bobbing from side to side as he walked. She should give herself away before he walked on too far, or she could be waiting, hunched up on the tree, all day. But he stopped a few yards ahead. He rummaged through one of the bushes, then walked north, parallel to her position.

A twig crunched behind her. If Henry was ahead, what could be coming toward them from that direction? A deer, or one of the prowlers from the previous day? She twisted her head around to try to see in that direction, but the leaves blocked her view.

The steps continued their approach. She turned back to look for Henry, who was disappearing between bushes before her. Should she call out? It could spoil his game, only to find a deer looking for them.

Something rattled against the tree behind her. She twisted toward it, trying to see what might be out there. Then she jumped as something touched her shoulder. Her heart froze for a second before it began beating again.

"Caught you," Pat whispered.

She put her hand on her chest, where her heart was now pounding like a steam engine. "And you almost killed me." She pushed leaves out of the way to look into his face. "What are you doing here? Father said you had returned to the village."

He leaned against the tree alongside her. "I wasn't going to leave you all alone just because your father told me to. Who knows what's running around in the wood?"

"Perhaps you should. You have caused little but trouble while we have been here."

"If you want me to go, I will."

"Pat!" Henry called.

Pat stepped back. Henry stared at them from a few yards away, with a big smile across his face.

"I found her for you," Pat said. "Now it's your turn to hide."

"That is not fair. I was supposed to find her."

Hope was glad to slide out of her hiding place, as the rough bark was poking into her back. Pat brushed dirt from her dress.

"Your turn, Henry," she said.

"Two against one is not fair."

"We'll look for you together, then," Pat said. "That way it's really no better than one against one."

Henry frowned at him. He didn't seem convinced.

"Get on, then," Pat said. "Or I'll start counting and catch you still standing there scowling at us when I stop."

"And stay out of the ravine," Hope said.

Henry huffed, then ran into the wood. Hope turned away and began to count. Pat closed his eyes until she reached one, then they turned.

"Coming," Pat yelled. "Whether you're ready or not."

Hope took a big step toward where she had last seen Henry, but Pat grabbed her arm. "No need to rush," he whispered. "Don't spoil the lad's fun."

Was Pat really concerned about Henry's fun, or his own? She nodded anyway, and they strolled between the trees in roughly the direction Henry had run. He couldn't be difficult to spot, so long as he wore his hat.

"How did your uncle end up living here?" Pat said.

"He was wounded during the Afghan War, and the natives captured him. He lived among them for three years, before he returned to civilization, and a few more years in India before he returned to London. Soon after that, he moved out here and bought this house. The next time we heard from him was when he asked us to visit."

"Seems like a strange one to come out here and board the place up like that. Then chopping up those things in the cellar..."

"Something happened during the war. Uncle Howard would not speak of his experiences there to Father, but Mother insisted he tell her what had happened, as brother to sister. So, one day, he did. She has been reluctant to talk since, and has said even less since reaching the house. She has never even been able to look at a Bible since then without discomfort."

"Strange family. Maybe your mother takes after your uncle."

"I hope you are wrong, for then I might take after both of them."

"I don't think you take after either of them, miss. Or perhaps you take after your father. He seems as determined to make you do what he believes best as you do to do what you believe best."

"Father is more concerned that my actions may harm his family name than he is about my happiness. His business is bad enough already, and he fears losing contacts if we are seen to be disreputable, whereas I fear losing my mind if I have to be seen and not heard for the rest of my life. Father grew up on a farm and made his own way in the world, he does not want us to end up back there."

"Nothing wrong with living on a farm, miss."

The trees thinned out as they approached the edge of the ravine. The wood continued on the far side, with no sign that Henry might have gone that way.

"Do you think we will ever find Henry?"

Pat sniggered. "He's much better at hiding than you are. For all I know we might already have passed him."

"Do you think that we should continue looking? Or should we just admit we are beaten by a better man?"

"I think Henry is better at hiding than we are at finding."

"Henry," Hope shouted. "We give up. Come out and show yourself."

They stood for a moment and looked around the woods. Nothing moved, not even birds in the trees.

"Henry," she shouted again.

"I think he is too far away," Pat said.

What of her dream, and the creature chasing Henry? "If he is in the ravine, we should find him."

"We should sit here, and wait for him to find us."

Pat sat on the edge of the ravine, his legs down the slope. Hope adjusted her dress and sat at a ladylike distance from him. As she sat there, he slid across the grass until he was beside her, then reached out his arm and put it around her shoulder. He gently pushed her to the grass and kissed her. She greedily kissed him back, tasting his lips. He slid on top of her, his hand slid up her side, and she moaned as he grabbed her breast. She held his back and pulled him closer.

Henry would have to wait.

By the time Pat released her, the sun was low in the sky and the air growing cold.

"I should be going," he said. "And if you are out much longer, your father will be looking for you."

"And what of us? If you return to Graiguengal I will never see you again."

"Come with me, then. Your dad will expect us to go to Graiguengal, but we can go south instead. We can be long gone before he realizes we went the other way."

Early that afternoon, she had been eager to follow Pat wherever he took her, turning her back on her family without a thought. But that had been a fantasy, and now she must decide whether to make the fantasy real. Could she do it?

She wouldn't miss the house. Sad to say, she wouldn't much miss her parents. She would miss Henry, but her father would ensure he was treated well. She looked into Pat's eyes as he smiled at her. She couldn't say no. But there were some things she couldn't leave behind, like her journal.

"I must fetch my things, then I will meet you back here. We can leave as soon as I have them."

Pat brushed the dirt and leaves from her dress. "Don't be long."

"Find Henry for me and tell him that I will see him when I can. If he is not there already he must return to the house before he gets in trouble."

Then she strode toward the house.

Her stomach churned. She was committing herself to live with this man, who she barely knew. But could it be worse than the life she already had? Perhaps, between them, they could somehow earn enough money to live decently, or at least enjoy their freedom if they couldn't.

Her parents were in the hallway as she entered the house. Eliza rushed around in her nightgown, pulling open doors and staring into empty rooms.

"Stop this," William said. "You are only exciting yourself. Sit down and rest."

He turned to Hope as she approached. "Have you seen Henry?"

"No. We were playing hide and seek, but I did not find him. I thought he must have become bored and returned here."

"Before he left, Pat told me he saw the two of you in the ravine yesterday."

Her father was going to blame her for what Henry had done, whatever she said. But she no longer needed to care.

"Kerberos ran down there and we went to find him. I brought Henry back when we found Kerberos."

"Did you not hear me tell you to stay away from there?"

"Henry ran down before I could stop him."

"Mrs Phillips said he wanted to go back there today. Did you take him there?"

"I told him to stay away. I did not think he would have gone down there by himself. I still do not."

Could he have returned to the tunnel, through curiosity, or because it would be a good place to hide? Perhaps he had gone there on his own, while she was indulging her desires with Pat? What if he fell down the tunnel and was unable to return? She would never forgive herself if she was responsible for his fate.

William walked along the hallway and into the dining room, calling for Mrs Phillips. Hope followed, and saw her scurry up the stairs and poke her head out of the door, wiping her hands on her apron.

"Have you seen Henry?" William said.

"Not lately, Mr Hodges," Mrs Phillips replied. "I've been busy with the deer."

Eliza strode into the room toward them.

"Where is Henry?"

"He is just playing a game," William said. "Nothing bad has happened to him, and we will find him shortly."

But something bad could have happened. Hope hadn't even mentioned the prowler to her parents, because she didn't want them to know she had ignored her father's warning. But if Henry was in the ravine all alone, it could have found him where she and Pat had failed.

William strode out of the front doors, and around the house to the lawn. Hope followed close behind.

"Henry! Where are you?" William shouted.

They waited, wandering the garden and shouting for him, but saw no sign of him and heard nothing. The sun was low in the sky, but there would still be some time before sunset. If Henry was outside, he should be returning for dinner.

Something bad had happened, and it was all Hope's fault. She should have warned her parents about the strange prowler the previous day, and she should have kept Henry out of trouble, rather than follow her foolish, childish desires for Pat. She had made an awful, irrevocable decision, and if only she could go back in time to change it, she would.

"I am so sorry, Father," she said.

William looked at his watch. "The sun should not be setting this early. This will make searching much harder than it should be."

They returned to the house, where Mrs Phillips was sitting in the lounge with Eliza.

"We must go looking for the boy," William said.

"He wanted to explore a tunnel down in the ravine," Hope said. "Perhaps he is stuck in there?"

"How could you have let him go?" Eliza said.

"I did not let him do anything. He must have sneaked off while we were playing hide and seek. Or hidden where we would not find him. Perhaps he is still hiding in the wood and will return once he realizes we have given up."

Mrs Phillips tipped Eliza's medicine into a cup of tea. "I'm sure they'll find him, ma'am. Boys like to cause trouble, it's in their nature. He'll be back by himself any moment."

"I will need a rope," William said. "In case I have to explore this tunnel."

Hope followed as he collected the rope and unlocked the study.

"Father," she said. "Yesterday, down by the stream in the ravine, something was watching us from the bushes. Kerberos chased it away, but we did not see what it was."

"In God's name, why did you not tell me?"

"I was worried that you would discover we had ignored you. We did not even know whether it was animal or human, we thought perhaps the tunnel was used by smugglers, and Kerberos would have scared them so they would avoid it while we were here."

"I hope to Hell that they have not hurt Henry." He turned to her with a sudden look of realization. "Perhaps smugglers drove Howard away. Or worse."

He took a revolver, and checked that it was loaded.

"Do you really need that?" Hope said. What if he ran into Pat as he waited for her? He might imagine that Pat was the prowler, and open fire. Or might fire because it was Pat.

He dropped the pistol into his jacket pocket. "If they have harmed Henry, then they will pay."

"Father, this is not the way to behave. We cannot shoot people just because we are scared for Henry."

"I have no intention of shooting anyone there who does not deserve it. But I will find Henry and bring him back if he is anywhere to be found."

He lit a lantern. Hope picked up a shotgun, and began to load it.

"What are you doing?" William said.

"I am coming with you."

"Your mother will need you while I am away, and I am not losing two children today. Besides, your ankle would slow me down."

"My ankle is fine. I have walked through much of the garden today."

"You will stay here."

He opened the door and made to step out. Hope put her arm in front of him, and he stopped to look at her.

"Why did you dismiss Pat?" she said.

"Henry heard noise downstairs last night, and, when he went to look, he saw you and Pat leave the cellar. Aside from the fact that you and Pat must have stolen my keys to enter the cellar against my express wishes, he said you looked flustered."

"I will say I was flustered. You have not seen what Howard keeps in his locked room."

"I will not have you entertaining any thoughts about a man like Pat. Besides, he has spent far too much time pursuing you, and far too little doing the job he was paid for. I have no need of a man who drinks when he should be working, even if he has no designs on my daughter."

He pushed her arm out of the way. "Now, let me do what I have to do. Comfort your mother."

He stepped out of the study door past her, into the hallway, and closed it behind them.

Hope finished loading the shotgun and slung it over her shoulder. It was heavier than she expected, and weight down her back. But not heavy enough to leave it behind. She prayed silently to God that she wouldn't have to use it, but, if the prowler was dangerous, at least she would have an opportunity to defend herself.

CHAPTER THIRTEEN

Hope took another lantern, and stepped out into the garden. She couldn't light it yet, or her father might see her. He was already well ahead, his own lantern glowing near the mounds as he strode past on his way to the ravine. Should she look for Pat first? She couldn't leave until she knew that Henry was safe.

Ah, Henry. If he had said nothing, Pat wouldn't have been dismissed, and she wouldn't have left him on his own. Their family was cursed, and every decision they made was the wrong one. No wonder Howard had disappeared, he was probably struck by lightning while practising his croquet, and was now watching the family comedy from a cloud high above them.

Kerberos followed her from the house.

"Be quiet," she whispered. He looked up at her as though he understood, then padded behind her in silence.

By the time they reached the ravine, the sun was low enough in the sky that the whole area was in deep shadow. William had clambered down the slope to the stream. Should she tell him that Pat was waiting for her? Perhaps they would find Henry stuck somewhere in the ravine, and return him to the house, then she could pack quickly and leave.

As William explored the ravine below, Kerberos and Hope walked back along the edge toward the forest, where she had last seen Pat. She walked as far as she could, but saw no sign of him. Hopefully, he was in hiding, or had already found Henry, and was taking him back to the house.

She turned to walk back to where her father had been, and lit the lantern. The sun was almost set, and she would soon have little choice. As she walked, she looked down into the ravine. She could see the swimming pool through the trees, and something lay on the ground alongside it.

Something red.

She scrambled down the slope, tearing her dress on tree branches, and forced her way through the bushes to the pool. Piled alongside it were clothes. Henry's. His new red hat was on top of the pile.

"Henry!" she shouted as she rushed to them.

No response came, and she could see no sign of him in the water. The mud beside the pool showed claw marks, and she could see a human footprint in mud beside the stream. Kerberos sniffed around the claw marks, then looked down the ravine.

This was the scene of her dream, just as she saw it.

"Please, God, do not let Henry suffer the fate I foresaw."

The bushes further down the ravine moved. She reached for the shotgun. But it could be William, Pat or Henry, as well as the prowler.

"What are you doing?" William yelled. "I told you to look after your mother."

He emerged from the bushes, and Hope picked up Henry's hat. "Henry was here. He must have decided to go swimming after we failed to find him."

William hurried toward her. "Oh, good God. I will have to search the pool for him."

"It becomes a bottomless pit a few feet from the edge. If Henry is down there you will never find him."

He turned to her. "How would you know that?"

"Henry and Pat went swimming here before."

"And they told you the pool is bottomless?"

She sighed and stared at the ground. "I joined them, and I almost drowned when I stepped into the pit. Perhaps there is a bottom, but I did not find one."

"My God, is there no depth you will not sink to in your quest to ruin this family's reputation?"

She could have smiled at her father's unintentional joke, but the situation was too serious for humour.

"Perhaps he continued along the ravine to the tunnel," Hope said. And perhaps the creature caught him part-way, as it had in the dream.

"Without his clothes?"

"The prowler might have surprised him."

William looked at Henry's clothes, then down the ravine. "Where is this tunnel?"

She pointed in the direction he was looking. "Some distance that way. I can show you."

William glanced at the shotgun on her shoulder. "Do not use that unless I tell you to. I do not want to end my days shot by my own daughter, because she mistakes me for a prowling smuggler."

He led the way, with Hope in the middle, and Kerberos trotting at her heels to the rear. She checked over her shoulder regularly, in case Pat was behind them. If he was in front of them, her father might well shoot him now even if he didn't mistake Pat for the prowler. But why would he have gone that far? Could the prowler have found him, too?

William pushed the bushes apart ahead of them. "How far is it?"

"Another hundred yards, perhaps. We were following the prowler that Kerberos attacked."

The bushes moved. William raised his hand, and they stopped. "Henry?"

Nothing moved, but Kerberos lowered his head and growled. William moved on. Hope followed him, and saw no sign of Henry before they reached the tunnel entrance. She looked in. It was as dark and unwelcoming as it had seemed the night before.

William crouched and picked up something that lay on the ground by the entrance. He held out his hand, and tipped the contents of a bag onto it. A set of marbles.

Henry had been there after all.

William looked around them, and pointed to a nearby tree with a thick trunk. "We can tie the rope around the tree, then I will descend into the tunnel. Can you pull me up if I cannot climb by myself?"

"I can try."

"That will have to do. I hope we are wrong, and Henry is already back at the house waiting for us. Your mother will be distraught if anything has happened to him."

Kerberos growled again, and Hope followed his gaze. The bushes moved ahead of them. She stepped back, in case the prowler had returned.

"Henry?" William called. "Is that you?"

He took a step toward the bush, but Hope grabbed his arm. "The prowler was near here yesterday. Be careful."

William pulled away from her, and crept toward the bush, calling Henry's name. Hope heard movement behind them, and looked over her shoulder. Kerberos continued to growl at the bush William was approaching, and her heart beat faster. "I think you should come back."

He glanced at her, then pulled the revolver from his pocket as he approached the bush. He held up the lantern in his other hand, and she stepped forward to try to see what he was seeing. Then he pushed the branches aside.

A creature crouched there, staring back at him. One of the creatures from her dreams, and Howard's underground abattoir, scaly grey skin, long claws, wide mouth full of long teeth and small dark eyes. It snarled at William, and lunged forward.

His military training must have returned to him, as he stepped away from the attack. The claws still caught his right arm, tearing bloody gashes across the back of his wrist.

Hope dropped the lantern to the ground as she reached up to swing the shotgun from her shoulder. The lantern rolled, the glass broke, but the wick stayed alight.

Kerberos bared his teeth, and crouched to jump toward the creature. William was struggling to bring his revolver to bear. Hope grabbed Kerberos' collar, and pulled him back.

The creature lunged forward again, and one hand pushed William's revolver away as the claws on the other attempted to slash his stomach. William raised his other hand, and the light from the lantern shone directly into the creature's face.

It hissed and backed up, then swung its arms toward him as though trying to knock the light away. Hope raised the heavy weight of the shotgun to her shoulder.

"Step back!" she yelled. Two steps, and she could shoot without hitting him.

He stepped sideways, and the light shone away from the creature. It lunged for him again, and he stepped back to avoid the claws, swinging the lantern toward the creature as he did so. The lantern smashed on its back, spraying burning oil across its body.

The creature screeched and reared up. The shotgun slammed into Hope's shoulder as she fired both barrels, and William emptied the revolver into its chest. Blood sprayed from the wounds, and it fell to the ground, twitching.

Hope lowered the shotgun, and looked down at the creature. What had she done? She hadn't even fire a gun before, let alone shot anything, and had scarcely considered what she was doing until it was over. Now the creature was mortally wounded, and its dying eyes stared at her.

"Thank you," William said.

As the shock wore off, she stepped forward to see whether her father was badly hurt. Blood oozed from gashes on his arm, but he twisted his wrist and flexed his fingers, so the damage wasn't serious.

"I have had worse," he said. "And at least it did not ruin my favourite jacket." The angle of his arm at the time the creature attacked had pushed the jacket's cuff back, so it was untouched.

Hope glanced back at the creature. The twitching slowed and stopped as the last of its life left its body.

Stones and dirt fell around their feet. Something slid down the slope toward them. Hope looked up, as Pat scrambled down.

"What's going on?" he said. "What are you shooting at?"

William turned and saw him. His face grew red. "What in God's name is he doing here?"

Kerberos barked. Hope turned just in time to see a second creature creep from the bushes behind them, as Pat picked up her lantern.

"Pat!" she screamed, as the creature's claws lunged for him.

He yelled as the claws slashed his back. He turned and kicked it, then Kerberos barked and rushed forward. For a second the creature was stunned, and Pat swung the lantern into its face. It screamed too, as broken glass cut its cheeks and burning oil engulfed its head, then ran back up the ravine on all fours with Kerberos nipping at its ankles.

Hope hurried toward Pat, as fast as she could in her dress. Blood ran down his back, from the deep gashes the claws had left there.

"Leave him," William said. "I will not have him back in the house."

"Then I will stay with him. I will not leave Pat for these creatures. Neither would you if you had any compassion in your soul."

The bushes moved ahead and behind. A loud screech came from the tunnel.

"For God's sake, let us return to the house before more of these creatures find us."

They struggled up the slope, dragging themselves to the top. Pat was still strong enough to reach out a hand and help Hope up, as more of the strange creatures screeched at them from the bushes at the bottom of the ravine.

They hurried across the garden through the darkness. Hope didn't want to look back and see what was following them, and didn't need to, because she could hear the screeching creatures behind them. What had been one or two screeches grew to a cacophony as one blended into another.

Eliza stood at the door, holding her own lantern.

"Get inside," Hope yelled, then regretted doing so as the shout used up air she needed to run. Her heart was pounding, and her breathing could barely provide enough air to keep her legs moving, not to mention drag her dress across the lawn. She wanted to stop to rest, but the horrific screaming seemed ever closer. If she didn't reach the door in the next few moments, she never would.

"What is it?" Eliza said.

Hope reached her first, and grabbed her arm. William and Pat followed behind, William panting hard, and Pat struggling with his wounds. Kerberos trotted alongside Pat.

"Mother, we must go into the house right away."

"Where is Henry?"

William reached them. "Come on, Eliza," he said, his breathing strained, and grabbed her arm. They pulled her back toward the house, Pat and Kerberos following.

The creatures appeared from the darkness, then stopped as they reached the circle of light of Eliza's lantern. They spread out around it, hissing, and slowly creeping forward. Were they scared of the light? Or unwilling to be the first to attack them, and suffer the fate of their comrades back in the ravine?

"Hurry, Mr Hodges," Pat yelled.

They pulled harder, dragging Eliza toward the door, against her will. She struggled.

"Let me go," she said. "I must find Henry."

"Hope!" Pat yelled.

She glanced back as one of the creatures raced toward her, while the others swung their arms and squealed as they watched its attack.

Pat ran toward it, and threw himself forward to grab its leg. Kerberos ran too, and Pat and the creature rolled across the ground as Kerberos tried to bite it.

"Get your mother into the house," William said.

Hope pulled Eliza behind her. Eliza's complaint had stopped now that she saw the creatures, instead she stared at them with her mouth open. She must have realized that she couldn't go looking for Henry that night.

Hope pulled her into the study. If only she could slump down in the chair to catch her breath, she would. But the creatures wouldn't give her that chance any time soon.

She glanced out of the door, and saw Pat dodging the creature as its teeth snapped at his face. Kerberos lunged at the creature's neck, but it threw out an arm, and his teeth planted themselves in that instead.

"Back, boy!" William yelled, then grabbed Kerberos' collar and pulled him away. He tried to pull Kerberos toward the house, but Kerberos struggled against him, trying to jump and attack the creature again, as Pat tried to stay out of its reach.

William released Kerberos, and ran for the house. Kerberos jumped at the creature's back, his claws tearing at it, and his jaws snapping at its neck. The creature turned from Pat for a second, and he swung a punch its way, his fist smashing into its jaw with a horrible crunching noise.

"Pat!" Hope yelled, then grabbed Eliza's lantern, and ran to help him. William grabbed her arm, and tried to pull her back toward the house, but she twisted from his grip.

She shone the light toward the creature's face, and it closed its eyes and turned away for a second. Pat heaved against its weight, and threw it into the bushes. It briefly lay stunned, but soon twisted around and climbed to its feet. Pat began to hobble toward the house. Kerberos jumped up at the creature, and wrapped his jaws around its neck.

The other creatures were moving, dropping to all fours to run toward them, braver now they had only a wounded man and a girl to face them, with no weapons other than the light of the lantern.

CHAPTER FOURTEEN

"Get back!" Pat shouted as Hope ran toward him. The creatures howled as they raced across the lawn.

She reached him, and grabbed his hand to pull him toward the house. His right leg was gashed from the creature's attacks, and, every time he put his weight on it, he grunted with pain. She put his arm around her shoulder to help support him as they made for the door. Kerberos barked at the approaching mass of creatures for a second, then decided to join them.

William stood at the door, holding one of the muskets. He raised it, and Hope glanced behind her. The first of the creatures was almost upon them, with more close behind. The musket boomed, and the creature tumbled across the lawn, a gaping, bloody hole in its back.

She was gasping for breath again when they reached the door. Kerberos squeezed past them as he raced inside, and they followed close behind. William slammed the door shut, and slid the bar into place. He fumbled with his keyring, then locked it. Kerberos crouched by the door, and growled.

Hope helped Pat into the chair. "How are you?"

He half-smiled. "I've been better. Thank you, miss, you saved my life there."

She turned to William. "You would have left him outside."

He ignored her, and put his hand on her mother's shoulder.

"Eliza, go to your room."

Eliza looked around the study. "Where is Henry?"

William took her arm, and turned her toward the inner door. "I will tell you later, in your room. Wait for me there."

Eliza nodded, and walked toward the hall.

Hope jumped at a loud crash outside the window. With a smash, the glass broke, and a grey clawed arm reached between the bars, dark eyes glaring through the window beside it.

William propped the musket against a chair, took the other revolver from Howard's gun cabinet, and crept to the window. The creature screeched at him through the bars, and swung its arm to try to grab him.

He aimed carefully, then fired one shot. Blood and gore erupted from the creature's head, and it fell back. Hope would have felt sick, if she hadn't seen so much in a short time.

William threw the keyring to Pat. "Since you are here, you can check that the other doors are locked, and the windows are secure. Hope, come with me."

Hope's ears were still ringing from the boom of the gunshot in the confined space, and she could barely make out his words. The guns had sounded loud enough outside the house, and even worse inside.

Pat nodded, and climbed to his feet, then he hobbled into the hallway. William took his musket, the two revolvers and another musket from the gun cabinet. He handed a musket and the empty revolver to Hope, along with a bag containing paper cartridges.

"Bring these."

Glass broke in the dining room, followed by screams. She left the guns on a chair as they raced toward the noise. Two of the creatures were battering themselves against the window bars, their arms reaching through the broken windows. Clawed hands trying to grab Mrs Phillips as she swung a heavy frying pan in their direction.

William raised his revolver, aimed, and shot both of them. They fell back from the window, and Hope rushed around the table toward Mrs Phillips.

"Are you all right?" she said, unable to think of anything more reassuring to say in such unusual circumstances.

Mrs Phillips stopped swinging the frying pan, but otherwise said nothing, merely staring at the windows. Hope would have felt the same way if she hadn't already seen such peculiar sights around the house that this now seemed normal.

"Mrs Phillips," William said.

She turned, and stared at him, lips quivering.

"Go to the kitchen, and keep the door closed."

Pat hobbled through the door. William pointed toward Mrs Phillips. "Look after her." Then he strode out into the corridor.

As Pat passed, he grabbed Hope's hand, and squeezed it.

"How is your back?" she said.

"Hurts like buggery, to be honest."

"When we have a moment, I will help you bandage it." She looked into his eyes for a second, then followed her father into the hallway. If she hadn't run out to help Pat, would he really have locked the door and left Pat to those creatures? Perhaps he still would.

Eliza was walking along the hallway toward them, from the stairs. William grabbed her.

"What is going on?" she said.

William tried to turn her around. "Go upstairs, my dear, wait in the bedroom."

"What is all that noise? Where is Henry?"

"Go upstairs, lock the door and wait for me," he said. Eliza was still standing at the bottom of the stairs when they hurried back into the study.

"Load the guns," William said. Hope picked them up, and began to do so.

William crept to the broken window, and looked out. He stared into the darkness as Hope worked, and her curiosity soon got the better of her.

"What is out there?"

"Another of the creatures is hiding by the tree, watching me watch it. The others are nowhere to be seen. We seem to have discouraged them for the moment."

She finished loading a shotgun, then began to work on the muskets. "Do you think we are safe?"

"With dozens of those creatures living near the house? I would say not. But they do seem too disorganized to launch an attack that we could not fend off."

"And Henry?"

"I do not want to think of what could have happened to Henry. I pray that he has found somewhere to hide where these things cannot reach him."

For all his words, he didn't seem to have much hope in his voice. Nor did she. If Henry was outside in the gardens, then the creatures must have found him. If only she had looked after him that afternoon, rather than spend her time with Pat, he would still have been with them. If he didn't return, she would never forgive herself.

Something scraped against the outside of the study door. They both turned toward the sound. Then a loud thump came from the door, followed by more scraping and thumping.

More glass smashed elsewhere in the house. William grabbed a musket.

"Come on," he said.

They left the study, stepping out into the hallway. Hope carried the guns, and a bag of cartridges and caps. More glass was breaking, the noise coming from the lounge.

William slammed the study door, and tossed the keyring to her. "Lock it," he said, then strode toward the lounge.

For a moment, she felt an insane urge to return to the study, and hunt through Howard's things to see if the books would tell them what these creatures were. He had known about them, and must have some idea of where they came from, or how to stop them. But she found the study key, and locked the door. A boom echoed around the hallway, and she turned to see William firing the musket through the doorway into the lounge.

"Revolver!" he yelled to her, then one of the creatures stepped through the door. William slammed the butt of the musket into the creature's chest, and pushed it back.

Hope ran across the hallway. The creature stepped forward again, and she could see another pushing its way through the broken window from the garden. Without even thinking, she raised the revolver, and fired past her father. The noise was so loud that the shock prevented her from firing again. Blood oozed from the creature's forehead, its eyes opened wide for a second, then it fell to the carpet.

William grabbed the revolver from her hand, and aimed at the other creature. It dropped to all fours, and lunged behind a nearby chair, but William fired twice. Two holes appeared in the chair, and a lifeless thud came from behind it.

More clawed hands bashed against the outside of the other windows, and broken glass fell to the carpet. William pulled the door closed, took the keys from her, and locked it. Pat hobbled along the corridor toward them.

William handed her the revolver. "Reload the guns." Then he looked at Pat. "Follow me."

A large chest of drawers stood up against the wall near the dining room. As Hope worked, they dragged the chest in front of the door. Just in time, as the creatures had begun to bang on it from the far side.

"Is there anything else to block the door?" William said.

Pat shook his head. "Not that I can think of. The dining room table is too heavy, and the cupboards we could move are locked away in the study and lounge."

Hope heard faint rattling, and looked past them. Mrs Phillips approached them, with a tray, cups and a tea-pot upon it.

"I thought you'd all like some tea," she said.

The banging stopped, as though the creatures had decided they would be unable to force their way through that door. Hope took a cup from the tray, and Mrs Phillips filled it for her. She drank the hot tea quickly, glad of some refreshment after the recent excitement.

William took the shotgun, and a revolver from her, and handed them to Pat.

"Have you checked the other doors and windows?"

"Most of them, sir. The screaming distracted me."

Mrs Phillips handed a cup to William, and he drank.

"Check the others," William said. Pat nodded, and William watched him hobble away. "Then stay down here and deal with any creatures who try to get in. We will stand watch over the gardens from the roof."

They handed the cups back to Mrs Phillips. "Take some tea to Mrs Hodges," William told her. Then they climbed the stairs, which seemed to go on forever ahead of them. Eventually, they entered the attic, and found the door which led out onto the ledge around the roof.

Thunder cracked from the coastline. Dark, wet spots splattered on the roof where rain was beginning to fall. Perhaps a storm would discourage any further attacks? They leaned over the battlements, and looked down into the garden. Hope could see no sign of more creatures.

Then they heard a thud from the front of the house, and raced around the ledge to see what was there. One of the creatures was bashing its head against the front door, a futile act, given the work Howard had done to fortify it.

William raised the musket, aimed carefully, and fired as the creature stepped back from the porch. Blood sprayed from the creature's back, and it collapsed on the stairs.

He handed the musket to Hope. "Reload that."

She handed him the musket she carried, and took his. As he turned back to look over the battlements, she crouched, and began to reload it. The rain was falling faster, and she covered the powder flask as well as she could, to keep it dry.

Then she heard smashing glass from the corner of the house, around the dining room. William rushed to the corner, raised the musket, and fired again. The loud squeal told her that he had hit another of the creatures.

She handed William the loaded musket, and began to reload his. A creature screeched down below. She glanced through the battlements, and saw it staring up at them from the garden. A booming shot came from below, as Pat fired the shotgun through a window. The creature squealed as the shot hit it, but stumbled onward toward the house.

William raised his musket. He fired, and dirt sprayed into the air where the ball hit the ground just behind it. He turned to Hope, and held out the empty musket to exchange for the loaded one, but she raised it to her shoulder and aimed. She was about to fire when William grabbed the barrel, and pulled the gun away from her. He swung it to his shoulder, aimed and fired in a few seconds. The shot hit the creature's leg, and it fell to the grass, rolling onto its back and squealing.

He handed her the musket. "Hurry, we should finish off that one."

She began to reload both muskets. As she did so, the creature's squeals stopped, and were replaced by a low moan.

"Not such a bad job," William said. "Perhaps we have killed enough of them to have scared the majority away for now."

"I hope so. If they come to the house in a mass I do not think we can stop them."

"The house is secure, and we have God on our side."

"Do you think they killed Uncle Howard? They must be the reason he barricaded the house."

William shook his head. "He built a good defensive position, then left the house, and locked the door behind him. They clearly never broke in, or we would have seen the damage."

"Perhaps he tried to reach the village. They might have caught him on the way."

"Hush. Let us not make such morbid talk when we have no proof that Howard is dead."

William stood, and raised the musket Hope had reloaded. She peered over the battlements as she finished the other, and saw another creature creeping across the lawn, toward the house.

William fired, but the shot went wide, smacking into a tree behind it. The creature hissed, and began to run.

She traded muskets with William, and began to reload the one he had just fired, watching the creature on the lawn when she could.

It didn't head directly toward the house as she had expected. Instead it turned toward the wounded creature. William raised the musket, and aimed. For a moment the creature sniffed around the wounded one.

"Wait," Hope said. "I want to see what it does."

William lowered the musket, stood beside her, and looked down himself.

The creature reached down, and touched the body, as though checking it was alive. A pool of blood surrounded the wounded creature's leg, and its moans had become faint squeals. For a moment, despite the creatures' murderous attacks on them, Hope almost felt pity that they had killed its friend.

Then the creature lowered its head, and bit a chunk of meat from the wounded creature's leg. It sat back on its haunches, and began to chew.

William fired. The creature's head spurted blood, and it fell dead beside the other. Hope handed him the other musket, and he put the wounded creature out of its misery.

"Do you see any more of them?" William said.

"Not this side."

She took the muskets, and began to reload while William looked over the battlements. Seeing nothing, he took out his pipe and lit it.

"Father, Uncle Howard had parts of the creatures in the basement. We found a hand just like those of these creatures."

He stared at her. "You knew of these creatures before we went to the ravine?"

"We knew that Howard had been dissecting something. We had no idea that they lived here."

William opened his mouth as though to shout at her, then raised his hand and shook his head. "We are alive and the house is secure, for now at least. Tomorrow we must make our way back to the village."

"What about Henry?"

William looked down. "He will be hiding, and our best chance to help him is to bring enough men from the village to clear these things out for good. For now, we must try to protect all sides of the house until morning. If they continue to attack in ones and twos, then we will have no trouble."

"You think Henry is alive?"

"I will not allow myself to believe otherwise, until I see evidence of his death. He is a clever boy and would not allow them to catch him. He can fit into many places where these creatures cannot."

"We saw no sign of his body in the ravine, if that was where he went. If he was down there he may have descended into the tunnel. He could even now be making his way to the house."

Hope hadn't even considered that thought, until it came to her on the roof. Her father must have realized the implication at the same time she did.

"As soon as we can," he said, "we should check the cellar, in case Henry has found his way here through a tunnel."

William walked around the roof, and Hope kept an eye on her side as she reloaded. She saw no further movement. Perhaps, for the first time since they ran into those creatures, they were safe? Most of them must have returned to the ravine, when they saw the first of their brothers shot.

Then she heard a loud thumping from the garden, and the crack of wood breaking. A horse whinnied in the stables, then another. She raced around the roof to get a better view.

Loud crashes and neighs filled the night air. One of the horses kicked out a plank from the back of the stable with its hooves. Another kicked the stable door, and broke away one of the hinges. Then the night went quiet, other than squeals and grunts.

Then silence.

The broken stable door swung open, and a creature emerged with a large chunk of bloody meat in its mouth. It stopped and sat outside, grabbed the meat with its hands, and held it while it leisurely chewed.

William raised a musket and fired. Blood exploded from the creature's head, and splattered over the stable wall. It fell to the ground on top of the meat. Another creature looked out the door, blood smeared across its face, then disappeared back inside the stables. She heard more thuds against the wood, and then a loud, extended squeal that made her skin crawl.

Thumping came from below, then gunshots. They ran around the ledge toward it, until they were directly above the front doors. Even before they got there, she could tell from the noise that the creatures must be trying to break in again. They looked over the parapet, but the porch blocked their view of what was happening. From the amount of noise they were making, a group must be attacking together for the first time, and staying close to the house so they couldn't shoot.

They raced down the stairs to the hallway, then toward the door. As the creatures banged on the outside again and again, it shook, despite Uncle Howard's reinforcing efforts. Pat crouched nearby, reloading his revolver. Kerberos stood with his front legs on the door, barking at the slits, and snapping at any clawed fingers which poked through them.

Hope looked through the slits, and saw the eyes of several creatures staring back at them. William pushed his revolver into the slit, and she pushed her fingers into her ears just in time to block some of the noise as he shot one in the face. The creature fell back.

The thuds from outside grew faster and frenzied. William moved to the other slit, and fired at another of the creatures. It squealed, and the banging slowed, then stopped. Another screeched outside and ran from the door. William shot it in the back, but it continued running and vanished into the darkness.

She struggled with powder and caps to reload the revolver as fast as she could. Then they heard breaking glass.

Then a scream.

CHAPTER FIFTEEN

William and Hope ran along the hallway toward the noise. The screaming came from Mrs Phillips' room. Hope reached it first, grabbed the handle, and tried to open the door. It was locked from the inside.

William banged on the door. "Mrs Phillips?"

All they heard in return was squealing and screaming.

He banged again. "Mrs Phillips!"

Pat hobbled along the corridor. William held out his hand. "Give me the keys."

Pat threw the keyring to him, and William flipped through it until he found the key to the door. He unlocked it, and pushed it open.

Pat pushed past Hope, and he and William barged into the room. The windows were broken, and two of the metal bars had been pulled loose.

Mrs Phillips lay on the bed, and one of the creatures chewed on her body. As it saw them, it turned its head, jaws covered in blood.

Hope turned away, not wanting to see more. She heard the creature snarl, then the loud report of revolver and shotgun as both Pat and William fired. It squealed.

She heard another scream, this time from upstairs. It could only be her mother. Her father pushed past her.

"Eliza!" he shouted, as he rushed toward the stairs.

Hope followed. Please don't let them find her in the same state as Mrs Phillips. She reached the landing and ran along the upper hallway toward her parents' room. William fumbled with the keys as he tried to find the one that would open the door. A loud crash and a scream came from inside the room.

"Hurry," Hope yelled.

Finally, the correct key twisted in the lock, and he managed to open the door. Pat caught up as they rushed in.

A creature stalked Eliza around the room, teeth exposed and jaws snapping. She held it at bay with a two-legged chair, the other two legs broken in half. The creature swung its clawed hand at her, bashing the remains of the legs from the chair. Two windows were wide open, and, with no bars outside, it had been able to climb in that way.

William and Hope raised their guns. The creature jerked as they emptied the revolver and musket into its body and head, blood and gore spraying across the room as it fell backwards onto the floor. The muzzle blast boomed in Hope's ears, and she could hardly hear William as he called to Eliza.

"Eliza, are you all right?" he said again, this time his words just audible over the ringing in Hope's ears.

"It banged on the window. I thought it was Howard," Eliza said. She stared at the mess the blood had made on the carpet. "We must clean up all this before Howard comes home."

As the ringing in her ears died down, Hope heard scraping noises outside the window, and crossed the room to investigate. Spray from the rain storm flew into the room through the open window, and lightning flashed outside above the woods. A creature was climbing the drainpipe, which must have been how the other had reached her parents' room. It hissed at her. She turned the musket around, grasped the warm barrel and smashed the butt into its face. Bone crunched, and the creature screeched and shook its head.

Its hands grabbed the nearest bracket holding the pipe to the wall. She raised the musket to hit it again, but the creature lurched back. The bracket must have been loose, because the creature's grip pulled two of the screws from the wall. Its dark gaze met hers for a second, then the drainpipe gave a metallic screech as the last of the screws pulled free. The creature's weight pulled the drainpipe backward, more brackets tore away from the wall below them, and it fell down and down toward the lawn. It smashed backward onto the grass, and the drainpipe crashed down on top of it. It whined for a moment, then lay still.

Hope silently thanked Pat for being so bad at his job.

Eliza sat on the bed. The garden below was dark and empty, with no sign of more creatures. Hope closed the window and sat on the bed beside her mother.

"Where is Henry?" Eliza said, seemingly having forgotten her recent adventure.

"I do not know," was all Hope could say. He must have fallen prey to the creatures, but she didn't want to be the one to tell her mother. Particularly if it was her fault.

"I want to see him."

William leaned over them. "We will go and find Henry in the morning. For now we must ensure we survive the night."

Eliza stared at the body of the creature on the ground, now apparently remembering what had happened. "Are they gone?"

William nodded. "We seem to be safe for the moment."

Pat hobbled across the room as Hope poked the creature's body with the musket barrel. This was the first time they had seen one up close without it trying to kill them. Pat crouched over the body.

"What is this thing, Mr Hodges?" he said.

"Nothing that should be on God's Earth."

Hope could certainly agree. The colour and shape of the body showed it was the same creature Howard had dissected to make his collection in the cellar. What perverse reasons was he studying them for?

The back of Pat's shirt was soaked through with blood from his wounds. He reached out and rolled the body over. It was clearly male, like the others they had seen so far.

"This one can join the rest," William said.

"Perhaps we should examine it," Hope said. "We might learn something about them."

"Examining them does not seem to have helped Howard. Live or dead, I do not want these things in this house."

William opened the window, then lifted its arms. Pat took its legs. The head dripped blood and gore onto the carpet as they carried it toward the window. They grunted as they lifted it to the window sill, then pushed. It scraped against the frame as it slid out, then tumbled to the ground outside.

William breathed deeply as he recovered from the exertion, then shut the window again..

"Pat, check Mrs Phillips' door is secure, then guard the ground floor."

Pat nodded, and hobbled to the door. William sat on the bed with Eliza.

He poured a large brandy from the bottle on the bedside cabinet, took a sip and handed it to her. Then he lit his pipe again.

"What was that thing?" Eliza said.

"I do not know. They followed us from the ravine."

"Where is Henry?"

"We found no sign of him, just those creatures."

At the news, Eliza drank from the glass. William pulled her to him, and stroked her hair. Thunder boomed outside the house, and rain battered the glass. They sat for a while, and Hope looked out of the window for any sign of the creatures returning. She should get away, and check on Pat.

"I should take a look on the roof," she said, knowing they wouldn't let her go if she told him where she was going.

After collecting some bandages from Howard's bathroom cupboards, she found Pat in the dining room, peering out of the windows. She stood beside him, and looked into the darkness, but saw nothing moving other than trees and bushes blowing in the storm. A flash of lightning lit the garden for a second, then darkness returned.

"Sit down, and take off your shirt," she said.

"Ah, miss, isn't that a bit forward?"

She showed him the bandages. "You need to cover those wounds before you bleed to death, and I do not think the creatures will return again tonight."

Pat put down his shotgun, and pulled off his shirt. He turned and sat on a chair, then leaned forward so she could reach his back. She sat behind him. His body smelled of hot sweat from the desperate exertions that night.

She held her candle close to his back, and examined the wounds. They had begun to heal, but were still bleeding, as every new exertion pulled them apart. They should have been stitched closed by a doctor, but they wouldn't have a chance to find one for some time.

"What do you think?" he said.

"I could try to sew them shut, but I do not feel I would do a good job. We can clean and bandage them for now, then find you a doctor when we escape from here."

"Do you really think we will?"

"If not, I feel I will go quite mad."

She meant that, too. These creatures must have been formed somewhere in the depths of Hell. She would go mad if she had to suffer many more nights with them banging on the windows and doors of the house. Without hope of escape, she might end her own life, sinful as that may be, rather than wait for the creatures to do it for her.

She put down her candle so she could pick up the alcohol. As she lifted the bottle and returned her attention to Pat's back, she saw a strange glow; the cuts themselves looked faintly green. She ran her fingers along one, in case the creature had spread some material across Pat's skin when it scratched him, but all she found on her fingers afterwards was blood, while the cuts continued to glow.

"What is it?" Pat said.

Should she even mention the oddity, when she had no idea what it might mean?

"Nothing. I do not think the wounds are too bad."

She poured alcohol onto a cloth. "But this will hurt when I clean them."

"Not as much as the claws did, I hope."

She ran the cloth over Pat's back and injured leg, the smell of alcohol floating into the air.

He winced. "Ah, I could do with some of that to drink."

Having cleaned the wounds, she began to bandage them. "Do you think they will come back tomorrow?"

Pat shook his head. "I think we scared them away."

Unlike her father and Howard, Hope wasn't an expert on military tactics, but clearly the creatures weren't either. They were lucky the creatures showed no more intelligence in their attacks than a hungry animal. Perhaps they had grown used to attacking the house where only Howard was there to protect it, and thought the family would be as easy?

"They only attacked us a few at a time," she said. "If they had attacked all around the house we would have been lucky to fight them off."

CHAPTER SIXTEEN

Before Hope slept that night, she took the opportunity to bring her journal up to date. It was better than sleeping, where the creatures might return and surprise her, or she might dream worse nightmares than ever before.

Pat snored beside her on the floor as she wrote, under a blanket she brought from her room to keep them warm in the cold night air. Eventually, she put the last word on the page, and, as her eyelids could barely stay open, she had to join him.

But she had little time to dream. Her father's shouts jolted her from her sleep shortly after sunrise. He grabbed Pat's shoulder, pulled him to his feet, then punched him.

Pat swung back at William with his fist, but William swung the butt of his musket into Pat's stomach.

"Stop it!" Hope shouted. "What are you doing?"

William turned the musket, and pointed the muzzle toward Pat. His face was red, and his eyes glared. She could smell brandy on his breath.

"Touch my daughter again, and I will kill you myself."

Hope reached out, and pushed the musket barrel away. Pat charged toward William, and punched him in the face.

"Will you two stop fighting?"

The musket fired, and the bullet ploughed into the wall by Hope's head. Her ears rang, and pieces of plaster hit her cheek.

The shock seemed to return William to his senses. Pat stepped over, and looked at her face. "Are you all right?"

"For God's sake, Father, he was not doing anything. I came down here last night to bandage his wounds and felt safer here than in my own room by myself."

That wasn't her only reason for staying there that night, but saying so would only make a bad situation even worse.

William looked set to hit Pat again, but her words seemed to calm him for a moment.

"I should check the house is secure, sir," Pat said.

William lowered his hand, and nodded. "We will leave as soon as we can, before those creatures return."

Pat looked at Hope. She nodded to him. He picked up the shotgun.

"All right, Mr Hodges."

William watched Pat as he turned away. He reached into his pocket and pulled out the cellar keyring.

"Wrap Mrs Phillips' body, then put her in the cellar. We cannot bury her before we leave, and I do not want these things getting to her while we are gone."

"Yes, Mr Hodges," Pat said. William gave him the keys, then Pat walked through the door, and closed it behind him.

William's face was red from the fighting and sweat ran down from his brow.

"What did you do that for?" Hope said.

"I told you to stay away from that man. I would not even have had him back in the house, if not for you. We would all be better off if he had left as I told him to."

"He was not doing anything wrong this morning, and he did his part protecting the house last night. We might all be dead without his help. If something happened, I was better off here with him than hiding upstairs."

William glanced out the window. "Try to find yourself some breakfast, it could be a long day."

"What will we do about Henry?"

William stared into the garden. "There is nothing we can do about Henry for now. We must save ourselves."

Hope left to find Pat. He was in Mrs Phillips' room, as her father had ordered. After the events of that night, she didn't feel much like eating, and seeing the half-eaten body on the bed eliminated any remaining thoughts. The windows were covered with boards, as either William or Pat had put them in place to cover the holes.

Pat dropped a rope by the bed, then pulled off the blankets, and dropped them on the floor.

"Do you need help?" Hope said. She wasn't sure she wanted to help, but she didn't want to be alone.

Pat studied her face, his eyes wide, and face still red from the fight with William. "You don't want to see this, miss. And your father wouldn't want you in here."

"I do not much care what he wants any more. I am not sure he does either. We have more important things to worry about than family squabbles."

Pat pulled the sheets from the sides of the bed, then lifted the edges, and wrapped the sheet around the body. Hope walked to him, trying hard not to look at the bloody mess that had been their cook and housekeeper the previous morning.

"I will feel worse if I have nothing to do."

Pat picked up a blanket, and placed it on the bed. Hope helped him pull out the sides until it was flat. Then he slid the wrapped body, the sheets now red and wet with blood, onto the blanket. Mrs Phillips' face was still uncovered, the mouth frozen into an eternal scream. Hope tried not to look at her as she helped him move her body across.

"You seem unaffected by this horror," she said.

"I've worked on a farm, miss. And I dreamed of worse things last night."

"What do you mean?"

"I dreamed I was one of those creatures, and a crowd of them were feasting on bodies in the tunnels. It was so real, I could have been there. Smelling their blood and tasting their guts made me feel sick, but I couldn't stop myself from joining in the feast."

"Was it Henry?"

"I don't reckon so, but it would have been hard to tell. There was a magic box that played pictures of people when I picked it up in my claws, a fair-haired girl screaming at us, and a grey dog trying to bite them."

"You are sure it was a girl?" Though Henry's hair was brown, in any case.

"From behind, I thought at first it was a boy in short trousers with his shirt off. But she had long hair tied up at the sides of her head, and, when she turned, she had a bosom with two scraps of cloth tied over it."

Should she be disappointed that, while he slept beside her, he dreamed of another girl? Or that he dreamed of being a hungry, cannibal monster? She kept the thoughts to herself.

"What happened?" she said.

"The creatures attacked her and the dog, and dragged her away. Your dad woke me before I saw what they did with her. I doubt they had anything good in mind."

They lifted the edges of the blanket, and wrapped them around Mrs Phillips, then sealed her in with the rope. Hope took hold of her feet as Pat took most of the weight, and they carried her toward the door.

"But there was something else, too," he said.

Hope looked into his eyes. After what he had told her, what could he have seen in his dream that he would be reluctant to talk about?

"There was a book," he said, keeping his voice low, "with a leather cover, all burned and smeared with blood. I picked it up, and flipped through it."

"And what did you find, that so disturbed you?"

"It was about us. Like someone wrote a journal, saying what had happened here."

Had he seen her journal in her room, or had his mind just made it up? Before Hope could think further, they entered the hallway, and walked toward the cellar door, Eliza and William shouted at each other near the stairs.

"Eliza, we must go," William said. "We cannot fight these creatures forever."

"I will not leave without my son."

If only they could return to Mrs Phillips' room, and leave her parents to fight in peace, but they had already carried the dead woman too far, and her blood was leaking through the blanket. A thin trail of tiny red blood spots ran back along the hallway toward the door.

"If he was out there with those creatures," William began, then his voice tailed off. He didn't need to say it twice, for Hope to understand. Henry would have little chance with dozens of the creatures hunting him.

"He is not dead," Eliza said. "I will not leave without him."

They carried the body toward the cellar, Pat taking the lead, as he held the keys. William glanced at them with eyes wide in horror. Eliza was too busy glaring at him to bother with them.

"We have to go," William said.

"You may go if you wish. I will stay and await his return."

"We will return with more men to eliminate these creatures and find him."

"Howard says that hunger drives the creatures mad, but they have not caught Henry and he will look for him."

"Where is Howard?"

Eliza strode toward the stairs. "He spoke to me from the garden when you went downstairs. He said we should leave, but I told him I will not go until he brings Henry back to us."

William followed her.

Pat unlocked the cellar door, and they descended the steps into the darkness. Blood dripped faster as they did so, leaving a trail of red spots on the stone.

"You all right?" Pat said.

Hope nodded. Would she ever really be right again? She was alive, and so was he, and that was really all she could ask for at that point.

"I think my father may be going mad."

Pat laughed, for the first time since the ravine the previous night. "He's just being a father. I'd do that if my daughter was messing around with someone."

"You have a daughter?"

"I don't think so. I don't have a wife yet."

"And how is that, Pat? You do seem popular with the village girls."

"Just ain't found the right one, miss. In the village, any how. But you have to keep trying, don't you?"

She nodded, ignoring his hint. Surely he had already tried most of the village girls, and was eager to 'try' her.

"In any case," she said, "I do not believe I am 'messing around' with anyone. I am not that kind of girl."

The faint echo of a laugh floated out to them, from deeper in the cellar. Was it just Pat's laugh returning to them?

"What is that?"

Pat moved faster down the stairs, his boots thumping on the stone. "Let's do this quick and get out of here."

Their job done, they rushed back up the staircase, and Hope sighed in relief to be out of that place. Mrs Phillips may not be any safer in the cellar than in her room, but she would certainly be cooler, and at least it would placate her father.

They found him in the kitchen. He held a shotgun over the end of the table, cutting down the barrels with a saw, sawing with his left arm, not his wounded right. He looked up at them.

"What are you doing?" Hope said.

"I must look for Henry."

"But you saw those things, sir," Pat said. "If they catch you outside you'll have no chance."

"We must do this, for Eliza's sake. She will not leave without him."

"Then I will go with you," Pat said. "Miss Hodges can stay here with Mrs Hodges."

Hope was about to interrupt, but William beat her to it. "I will not leave a woman and a girl alone in this house. Much as I hate to leave you in charge, I need someone who can look after them." He looked at Pat's leg. "In any case, your leg is still not healed."

"I will go with you, Father," Hope said. "You cannot go on your own, and Henry would not be lost if I had taken more care to look after him. And your arm is injured."

"She shouldn't be going out there with those things," Pat said.

William finished cutting through the barrels, then twisted the last vestiges of metal from side to side until they broke free. He slung the shotgun over his shoulder. "Give me the other gun."

Pat slid it from his shoulder and handed it to William. He placed the barrels across the corner of the table and began to saw.

"That won't protect you against those things for long," Pat said. "You can't do this."

"I have to," Hope said. "I will not let Father risk his life looking for Henry alone, when this is all my fault."

William cut the barrels of the shotgun short, and handed it to Hope. He walked to the stairs and climbed up to the dining room.

Pat turned to Hope. "Take care."

She kissed him. "I will."

William reappeared at the door, holding a canvas bag and two raincoats. "Pat, there are still planks in the cellar. Do what you can to strengthen the doors and windows, in case we have to stay another night. Hope, collect some candles and meet me in the study."

Pat glanced at her as he hobbled up the stairs. If he had tried, he could surely have convinced her not to leave the house with her father, but he said nothing. Surely neither of them was likely to return? If not for her guilt over Henry's fate, she would have turned back before she could leave. She loaded candles and other supplies into a bag, and slung it over her other shoulder, then climbed the stairs to find her father.

He was waiting in the hallway with the study door open, a coiled rope slung over each shoulder and a lantern in his hand. He handed the lantern to her to carry, and a raincoat which she put on. He was already wearing another.

She peered around the door frame into the study, expecting to see more evidence of the creatures causing damage during the night. Instead it looked just as they had left it, though the clocks seemed even less in time than before. The creatures must have abandoned their attempts to break in there, after they locked the door.

William closed the hallway door behind them, locked it, then slid the wooden bar from the outer door, and unlocked that. Hope fully expected one of the creatures to jump in through the doorway the instant they opened it, but outside was just a cold, wet day. William picked an umbrella from Howard's collection, and handed it to her.

Then he pulled his shotgun from his shoulder and stepped outside, scanning the garden. Hope opened the umbrella and followed close behind, then heard a whistle from above and looked up. Pat watched over them with a musket from one of the bedroom windows. William locked the door, then threw the keyring to him.

"Keep the doors locked until we return," he said.

They walked around the corner of the house, then toward the front doors. Pieces of drainpipe were scattered across the croquet lawn, but no sign of the creature which had been climbing it, or the one they had shot there.

"No bodies left at all," she said.

"They must have sneaked back and eaten the dead," William said. "Perhaps when we were asleep."

She shivered at the thought of these strange creatures eating even their own dead. The front door had fresh scratches, and some wood had splintered away. Other than that, there was no sign of the creatures they had shot. But something was smeared across the wall in blood. The rain had washed part of it away, but she could still just discern the word 'leave'.

She pointed it out to her father.

"Do you think Uncle Howard returned during the night to leave us a message?"

"It is probably just blood from the creatures we shot, and just happens to look like a word."

She stepped closer. The curves were rough, but certainly looked like letters. What if the creatures were smarter than they appeared? Or, at least, some of them were?

"What else could have done it but the creatures? Do you think they can write?"

William ignored the question. "We should check the stables."

They crept past the house and across the yard, looking for any sign of creatures lying in wait. The stable door was battered and cracked from the attack the previous night, and hung from one hinge.

"Wait here while I go inside to see whether anything is still alive," William said.

He pulled open the door, releasing the stench of blood and rotting meat. He stepped inside, and Hope followed anyway.

All that remained of the horses was a bloody mess strewn across the floor, and she couldn't tell where one of the bodies began and another ended. The creatures must have torn them apart, and spread their insides around the stables.

Feeling sick, she looked away and lowered her gaze toward the floor. The stallion's head lay on the ground beside the door, a hole gnawed in the skull.

William took her hand and led her back out. "We will not be riding anywhere. If we are to leave, we must go on foot, which will not help our chances."

He pushed the door closed behind them.

The fresh air helped to bring Hope's turbulent stomach back under control. "We only saw these creatures near the ravine. If they live there, then perhaps, once we are outside the walls of the estate, they will not attack us."

With no sign of immediate danger, they walked toward the house, though Hope glanced behind now and then to ensure no creature had decided to crawl up the well from below. She could see Pat in the window, still watching them.

"Kerberos!" he shouted.

From the corner of her eye, Hope caught sight of something moving, and turned toward it. Kerberos ran from the house, his tail wagging. He wanted to join their expedition, and he might come in useful.

She looked up at Pat. "How did he get out?"

Pat's smile became a frown as he realized her implication. "I don't know, miss."

"If he found a way to get out, then perhaps the creatures could use it to get in."

Pat nodded. "I'll take a look."

He disappeared from the window as they walked toward the ravine. Hope wished he was still there to help protect them, but she would have hated her mother to succumb to Mrs Phillips' sad fate because Pat didn't block a broken window.

"Do you think Mother has really seen Howard?" she said.

"I do not know what to think. If anyone could be hiding out here among these creatures and sneaking back to see your mother, it is Howard. Who can fathom his intentions?"

They reached the trees at the end of the garden above the tunnel entrance without incident. The creatures seemed to have other things to do, or perhaps the battle the previous night had worn down their resolve, or reduced their numbers enough that they had gone into hiding for now. In any case, they seemed to have returned to wherever they lived during the day.

"If they were scared of the lantern, then perhaps they will not trouble us so long as the sun stays up and we stay in its light," William said.

Hope nodded. "The prowler we saw was creeping through the bushes, out of the sunlight. And the other was in the wood when it ran into Pat."

Rain was still falling, and the ground was soaked through, so the slope was muddy and unstable. William took one of the ropes from his shoulder and tied it around a thick tree trunk, then dropped the loose end down the slope. It snaked through the grass and mud, and piled up near the mouth of the tunnel.

"Can you climb down with your arm injured?" Hope said.

William tested the rope. "If that is what it takes to find Henry, I will. I can rest when we are safely away from here."

He clambered down the hill to where the stream raced past the tunnel entrance, the level higher than they had seen before. A night of rain must have made its way down the ravine to the sea, forcing its way past the earth that had fallen from the slope.

William waved to her, and she closed her umbrella to grab the rope, then struggled to keep her boots from sticking in the mud as she scrambled down. Kerberos watched them from the top of the slope, running from side to side around the trees. Eventually he decided to join them, but, with no hands to grasp the rope, he just jumped out onto the slope. He tried to run, but his paws slid on the mud, his legs went out from under him, and he slid down past Hope into the stream. As she reached the bottom, he was shaking the water from his fur.

William picked up the end of the rope, and lowered it into the tunnel. He put the revolver in his jacket pocket.

"Give me the lantern, and bag."

Hope handed them to him, and he struggled to light the lantern in what little shelter the tunnel entrance provided. If anything, the rain was worse than when they left the house, and Hope was glad Howard had prepared for this weather. Without the raincoats, they would have been soaked to the skin by the time they reached the ravine.

Kerberos peered into the tunnel beside William's legs, and growled deep in his throat.

"Do you think the creatures are waiting for us?" Hope said.

"If I find any down there I will deal with them. Stay here and guard the entrance. I do not want them cutting the rope while I am below, because without it I almost certainly cannot climb back up."

Couldn't he leave the other rope with her, so she could lower it to him if he needed it? She looked up and down the ravine. She could see little past the bushes, which would provide excellent cover for approaching creatures, and little chance for her to escape if they crept that way.

"I do not want to stay up here hoping that those things do not come looking to eat me."

William glanced at the undergrowth, then looked into the tunnel. "You will have a much better chance here than down there. At least so long as the sun is up."

"Henry's disappearance is my fault, Father. I should be searching for him with you."

"You will stay here. If the creatures do return, and you and Kerberos cannot hold them off, make your way back to the house, then on to the village with your mother."

He tied the lantern to the bag, backed into the tunnel, and descended into it with care, as his shoes struggled to find grip on the wet rock. The lantern lit only a small section of tunnel around him, and the light grew dim as he descended. Kerberos peered into the entrance, but he showed no sign of following. He seemed to be demonstrating more intelligence than they were.

CHAPTER SEVENTEEN

Hope looked up and down the ravine again, peering into the deep shadows beneath the trees and bushes, where anything could be hiding. She couldn't stay there for long waiting for her father to return, even with Kerberos for company. She clung tightly to the shotgun every time a leaf twitched in the wind. She would go mad if she stood there for an hour, thinking every movement was one of the creatures preparing to attack.

William's descent seemed to take forever. How deep could the tunnel possibly go? Finally the rope went slack, and he must have reached the bottom.

Her dress was already wet, torn, and dirty from the mud and branches. She tore it further to ease her movement, then stepped into the entrance, holding on to the rope. She began to descend herself, taking one last long look at the world outside. Would she ever see it again? Kerberos stepped to the edge of the tunnel, and looked down to watch her as she descended.

Then her foot slipped on the wet rock. She clung tight to the rope, and strained her arms to hang onto it as she tried to regain her footing. For a moment, all she could hear was her rapid breathing echoing around the tunnel, until she found a solid footing on the rock and her heart stopped beating like a crazed drummer. She waited a few seconds to recover, before she continued.

Part of her wanted to look down and see whether she could spot the light of her father's lantern at the bottom. Another part didn't want to look down, because she didn't want to know how much further she would have to descend. Another part wanted to give up and return to the surface, but she could no more face the climb back up than she could the rest of the climb down. Nor could she hang there for the rest of her life.

She slipped again, lost her grip on the rope, then screamed as she slid down the last section of the tunnel and splashed into water at the bottom. She struggled to climb out onto drier land before the cold water soaked her to the skin and froze her arms and legs.

William grabbed her arm and pulled her up. "What are you doing?"

"I could not wait up there while you risked your life for my mistake."

He shook his head. "You will be the death of me, my girl." Then he held his finger to his lips and turned his head to look down the tunnel.

"I heard a noise," he whispered.

Hope looked into the tunnel, which led gently upward in the direction he was looking. A small stream ran into the rocks in the other direction, carrying away some of the water that had accumulated there.

But she could hear nothing other than the rapid tinkling of water running through the stream, and the slow, intermittent dripping of water from above them.

He slid the bag from his shoulder, and handed it to her. "If I could send you back up I would, but now I fear you are as likely to die in the climb as you are with me. Make yourself useful and find me some candles."

She reached into the bag and pulled out a bundle. William took them from her, and lit one from the lantern.

He ran his hand over the wall and brushed the dirt and stones away from a flat spot, then dripped some wax onto the rock and planted the candle on top to hold it in place. It wobbled, and he adjusted it until it held firm.

He lit another candle from that one, and handed the bundle back to her. "Place them as we go. They will show us the way back."

Hope held the candles in one hand, glad her father, at least, believed they would survive to return this way. His revolver clicked as he cocked it, and he walked along the tunnel holding the lantern high above him in his other hand.

"Come on, quietly."

They crept along the tunnel, and Hope tried not to make noise. Her wet legs were freezing in the cold, damp air, while her fingers were burning hot from the wax dripping down the candle she held.

Stones rattled down the tunnel behind them, then something splashed into the water. Hope turned and pulled the shotgun from her shoulder, ready for whatever approached them. William backed up against the wall and looked both ways, then nodded to her and continued creeping deeper into the tunnel.

She followed, but then heard a moaning noise from behind them. She looked around, but the candle barely lit the area she was in, let alone the rest of the tunnel.

Something scrabbled along the tunnel behind them, and she pulled back one of the shotgun's hammers with her thumb. The noise came closer, and William stopped, turning the lantern to shine the light down the tunnel. Two eyes in the darkness, stared at Hope.

With her heart beating fast, she squeezed the trigger. She stopped just in time as Kerberos ran out of the darkness, fur dripping wet. He barked and jumped up at her. She pushed him down, and lowered the hammer on the shotgun.

William turned back to look up the tunnel before them. "Keep the dog quiet."

Hope slung the shotgun again, held Kerberos' collar to stop him racing ahead, and followed William along the tunnel. It began descending, not as steeply as the entrance they had climbed down, but still taking them deeper into the Earth. Would it prove to be their tomb, as it may have been Henry's?

They planted more candles as they followed the tunnel. The further they descended, the more the walls looked like the black stone in the house and glowed with their own faint light, so they left fewer candles. As Hope stared at the wall, she could see faint threads of light brightening and then disappearing. She held out a hand and pressed her palm against the damp stone, which glowed warm around her fingers. She would have called for William to show him the odd behaviour, but he was already getting ahead of her.

At least they hadn't run into any of the creatures. Perhaps their arrival had scared them enough that they had retired to a safe distance? She still held little hope for finding Henry, but perhaps he could have found himself a safe hiding spot if he had come down there.

Faded red material coated the walls, in thick smears like a painting a child might make with their fingers. William stopped and lifted his lantern to examine it, while Hope stepped in close with the candle. The shape was rough and indistinct, yet still familiar. The towers and battlements of the house were obvious enough, even though the rest showed little detail. Flames rose from the woods and outbuildings, and large stylized representations of the creatures looked on. A larger creature with wings and horns towered above the house, with clawed arms raised above its head.

"Who could have made this?" she said.

William reached out and ran his fingers over the picture of the house. He lifted them to his face and studied them in the lantern light. "I have no idea. The paint is dry, so not Henry's work. Perhaps the creatures themselves?"

"What do you think it represents?"

"I had a dream like this shortly after we arrived. The house was on fire in the snow, and some creature was hunting for us. It could have been the Devil himself."

"You have had dreams about the house too?"

His face flicked toward hers. "I did not realize anyone else had. Between your behaviour and your mother's and the dreams, I have not slept much for the last few days."

She remembered the gossip among the villagers, about Howard worshipping devils. Could they have meant these strange creatures? Perhaps Howard had been working with them? The missing girl the villagers had spoken of may not have eloped after all.

"Who knows how far the tunnels go down into the bowels of the Earth," William said. "Perhaps all the way to Hell."

Hope shivered at the thought. "Then I hope that Henry is not there."

William turned to continue down the tunnel, and swung the lantern from side to side as he studied the walls. Hope could see more pictures of the creature and the house, but who could have made them? Particularly the picture of the house in the flames, as they hadn't seen any sign of a fire in the past they could have based the picture on. Perhaps it was an event they feared, rather than one they had seen.

Something crunched. Hope looked down, and lowered the candle toward her feet. She was standing on an old, gnawed leg bone. William turned and accidentally kicked a pile of bones that rattled around the tunnel. A human skull rolled along the tunnel and stopped in front of her, a hole gnawed in the top.

"Is that...?" she began.

William crouched and examined the bones and the other debris around them. He held up pieces of flint, the edges chipped away. "The bones are far too old to be Henry. Wherever he is, that is not him."

As they were beginning to run low on candles, they reached the end of the tunnel, which opened out into a large cave. The ground fell away ahead of them, becoming a narrow ledge leading off to the right. On each side of the tunnel mouth were tall sculptures similar to those Hope had seen in the cellar. They better resembled the creatures who attacked them the previous day, but some also had wings.

But they didn't have time to waste studying the sculptures. William held out the lantern, and they leaned out to look down, but all Hope saw below them was the darkest black of a pit that seemed to descend forever. William turned the lantern toward the walls, which bulged inward in a regular pattern as though made from a collection of huge ropes or cables leading deep into the Earth.

He placed the lantern on the ground and picked up a rock. He stepped toward the pit, took a good swing and threw it into the darkness.

It fell. Hope leaned over and listened. Perhaps they would never hear it hit the bottom? Finally, she heard a clatter echo from the walls. Then a crash as lightning sparked far below.

The blue light of the lightning illuminated the darkness for a split second, showing that they stood at the edge of a circular pit where the walls descended as far below them as they could see, and cable-like outcroppings of black stone intruded all around the perimeter.

"Did you see a tunnel on the far side?" Hope said. She had seen something there as the lightning lit the pit.

"I did not see much in that brief light. But if the ledge runs around the pit, we should follow it to ensure there is no other way out."

"We could drop more stones into the pit, to try to cause more lightning."

William shook his head. "We are lucky we did not bring those creatures flocking to us the first time. I will not risk it a second."

The sound of the lightning must have been heard by any creatures nearby. Perhaps the flash of light scared away any who contemplated looking for them.

"Give me the candles," William said.

Hope took the remaining bundle from her bag and handed it to him. He pulled some candles from the bundle, lit them, and placed them on rocks near the entrance, packing smaller rocks around the base to hold them against the cave wall.

He began to walk along the ledge. As he did so, the light of his lantern diverged from a straight line, as the ledge followed the curve of the cave.

"Stay here, Kerberos," she said.

He ignored her, and followed them anyway.

The ledge grew narrower as it passed around the curved outcroppings in the wall. William looked back at Hope, then turned sideways, his back to the wall, and crept past.

She tried to keep one eye on Kerberos as she followed. If they had to turn around and go back, any misjudgement could send them tumbling into the pit. The ledge widened after they passed the outcropping, and again at the next. She was relieved when it grew wide enough that she could turn away from the wall and walk forward along the ledge, so she wasn't looking directly down into the abyss.

Moments later, they found themselves on the far side of the pit, almost back at the dim light of the candles by the entrance, whose flames flickered in the turbulent air rising from the pit. Kerberos sat beside Hope, tail wagging, the only member of the expedition who seemed unconcerned by their position.

"If Henry fell in there, then he is gone," William said.

Unless they had missed a small tunnel in the darkness, this was as far as anyone could have travelled from the entrance in the ravine. If Henry had found his way into the tunnel at the ravine, they would have found him, unless he fell.

"Is there some way we can climb down to look for Henry?"

"In the dark? We could attach the rope to something, but I cannot imagine that Henry would even have tried to climb down, let alone succeeded," William said. He turned and held the lantern up as he looked around the pit.

Spikes on the outcropping not far from them would provide a solid enough place to tie the rope. But Hope could understand William's reluctance to simply descend into the darkness and hope they found something worth descending for before they reached the end of the rope.

"I think we have gone as far as we can," William said. "If Henry is alive, his fate is in God's hands now."

There must be a way down. If the creatures who attacked them came out of the tunnel they had followed, then they must have come from the pit. Hope knelt by the edge and lowered her head, until her eyes slowly became accustomed to the dim light that glowed from the walls. She saw it then.

She motioned to her father. "There is a tunnel some ten feet below us, leading into the wall of the pit. Could we climb down and continue our exploration?"

He crouched beside her and looked where she pointed. "Perhaps we should not give in quite yet."

He stood, walked to the outcropping, tied one end of the rope around the spikes, and lowered the other into the pit.

He looked at her. "I would tell you to stay here, but I am sure you will ignore me. This time, do not fall because there will be no-one to rescue you if you do."

He removed his raincoat and placed it on the ledge beside the outcropping. Then he handed the lantern to Hope, wrapped the rope around his body, and took a solid grip on it before he backed up to the edge. The spike he had tied the rope to was several feet to the side of the tunnel, and he wouldn't be able to drop directly down to it.

"If I reach the tunnel, I will try to tie the rope so you can climb straight down," he said, then stepped back off of the ledge and began to lower himself into the pit. The rope creaked as the fibres tightened and stretched under his weight.

In a moment, he lowered himself to a level alongside the tunnel, but was still unable to reach the entrance. He adjusted his grip, then pushed himself away from the rock with his feet and swung the rope toward the tunnel. It scraped against the ledge and the rough rock tore through the outer fibres. Hope opened her mouth to call down to him, but he swung one more time, and then he was in the tunnel.

The rope went slack, then shook a few times. William's head appeared at the tunnel entrance.

"Climb down if you are coming," he said.

She had been determined to do so. But when actually faced with the prospect of clambering down a rope into a dark abyss where all she could hope for if she fell was that she might die of fright before she reached whatever bottom the pit might have, did she really want to be an adventurer?

But William was looking up at her as he waited for her to join him. Her only other option was to wait on the ledge in the darkness for him to return, and hope that he would return, rather than be captured by the creatures... or worse.

Climbing down was less frightening.

She left her raincoat beside his, then adjusted her bag, tied the lantern to it, and took a deep breath before she began the descent. Kerberos watched her as she stepped toward the ledge.

"You will have to stay and wait this time."

He sat on the wet rock, as though he understood.

She stepped to the edge, then lowered her legs over the side beside the rope, glad she only had to descend a few feet to reach the tunnel. She took the rope in her hands, gripped tightly, and lowered herself down it, hearing her blood pounding in her ears as her feet scrabbled against the rock and her arm muscles struggled to hold her weight.

CHAPTER EIGHTEEN

Something grabbed Hope's legs. She twisted them for a second to break free, then looked down. William held on to them, and helped her into the tunnel. He had tied the end of the rope to another rock, so it would still be there when they returned.

If they returned.

He took the lantern and led the way.

"Should we leave candles?" Hope whispered.

"How many are left?"

She rifled through the bag, trying to make as little noise as possible as she hunted for them.

"Three."

"Then there is no point. Besides, I have no desire to stay down here any longer than we must."

He was right. Even without the fear of running into some of the creatures, Hope wouldn't want to leave Kerberos on his own for long, in case he did try to follow.

William crept onward, and Hope followed, watching the walls for any sign of tunnels crossing them, and behind for creatures following. She jumped with shock at loud crack from ahead, and the tunnel was lit for a split second with blue light.

"What was that?" she said without thinking.

"I have no more idea than you. But I wish I was moving away from it, rather than toward it."

They crept along the tunnel for five minutes that felt like an hour, and the cracks and flashes continued at seemingly random intervals. As they turned a corner, they could finally see the source as the tunnel opened out to overlook a cave. Below them, a raised platform of rock crossed a pit, leading to the far side of the cavern. In the pit were piles of bones, some of which appeared to belong to men, broken and gnawed.

"Could that be Henry?" Hope whispered.

"By God, I hope not."

Lightning flashed above them, where the creatures swarmed over intricate blocks of black stone hanging from the roof of the cave. More creatures than they had ever seen before. The glow from the stone was lighting the cave, and the stone blocks resembled the machines Hope had seen in her dream of the city in the ice.

"What are they doing?" she whispered.

"It could be some kind of steam engine. They are so busy dealing with the machines, that perhaps it explains why they did not bother with us."

Between the machines, a group of creatures crouched on a raised platform. One stood, just as a burst of lightning flashed between them. The lighting hit it, and it disappeared, as Hope had in her dream. Where had it gone? To the house, as she had dreamed? The other creatures hunched down, and turned away from the light.

A moment later, the creature reappeared. Its skin smoked and its body was thin and wrinkled as though aged years in a few seconds. Then it broke into flakes of flesh and burned bones, which fell to the ground from the platform.

"Thank God they do not have that for a weapon," William said. "We would stand no chance."

"I dreamed they once lived in a city in the ice, but moved underground from there."

"There is a theory that the world was once covered with ice, and the creatures who could not move south died from the cold. But, even if that is true, it must have been many centuries ago."

Something moved among the machines. A shiny, metal spider the size of a locomotive, with glowing eyes on the front of its head, crawled along the side of one. Its feet tapped against the stone as it moved down, then across the underside of the platform where the creatures stood. It disappeared from sight behind a machine on the far side. Was it one of the creatures she had seen in the drawings in Howard's study? Had Howard been down here too?

"Perhaps they have been below the estate for all this time," Hope said, "tending their machines? Biding their time until they can rebuild their city, as Mother suggested."

"We should leave. We have dawdled too long, and if Henry found his way down here then I fear his fate was no better than Mrs Phillips'. We will return and clear out this nest of demons when we have enough men to do so."

But he was too late. As Hope looked past him, one of the creatures on the machine glanced down, and stared straight into her eyes. It climbed to its feet and screeched at them.

William grabbed her hand, then led the way back along the tunnel. They hurried as fast as they could in the dim light of the walls and lantern. If they ran, they might run right out of the tunnel before they even realized they had reached the pit.

"Go first," William said, as the rope appeared ahead in the light of the lantern.

Hope wanted to wait for her heartbeat to slow after rushing from the cave, but the creatures would be following very soon. More might be waiting up above, but those behind would soon reach them in the tunnel.

She took hold of the rope and began to climb. William helped her up as far as he could, then trusted her arms to pull herself the rest of the way. Her shoulders felt as though her arms were pulling themselves from their sockets, and her elbows ached before she had gone a few feet, but she could push herself beyond the pain or fall into the pit. A moment later, she clambered onto the ledge and looked for signs of the creatures. All she saw was Kerberos, sitting patiently by the outcropping as he waited for them.

She called down to William, and his face appeared over the edge a moment later. He clambered onto the ledge beside her. At least they had travelled that far without being caught.

"Let us return to the house as fast as possible," he said, then picked up his raincoat and handed Hope's to her.

She heard a faint scraping noise below them.

Kerberos howled, and the sound echoed around the cave. It was answered by a ghastly cackle from below.

William stepped toward the pit. Suddenly he dropped his coat, grabbed the shotgun sling and pulled the gun from his shoulder. He pointed it down, and fired just as one of the creatures began to crawl out of the pit in front of them.

The creature fell back. The gunshot echoed around the cave and left Hope's ears ringing, and, as she stepped forward and looked down, a flash of lightning illuminated the pit. More of the creatures were climbing toward them. The creatures must have followed them from the tunnel to the cave, or climbed from other tunnels in the darkness beyond where she could see. They pressed themselves against the wall as the lightning flashed, then, as darkness fell again, they resumed their climb toward the ledge.

Stones rattled down the sides of the pit as they climbed up. More stones rattled from above. William raised the lantern. Light reflected from the eyes of more creatures climbing down the cable-like ridges on the walls.

Why hadn't she imagined there could be more tunnels above them? Could Henry have climbed up and found a place to hide? If so, he should have heard them and climbed down, or at least called out. The whole cliff must be full of tunnels. Did they all contain horrors like those they had seen?

Another creature clambered onto the ledge on the far side of her father. He raised the shotgun, and fired the other barrel, sending it flying back into the pit.

Hope stepped toward him, and caught movement in the corner of her eye. A candle fell into the pit as one of the creatures climbed onto the ledge, and, as it fell, it illuminated more of them below before going out.

William knelt and began to reload the shotgun. "We must leave now or we stand no chance."

If they still had any chance. One of the creatures had climbed onto the ledge and crept toward Hope. Kerberos crouched by her side, growling.

William poured powder into his shotgun barrel.

"Shoot it."

The creature crept closer, hissing. She raised the shotgun and aimed at it. Should she shoot while it was too far back to knock her off the ledge if she didn't kill it, or wait until it was close enough that she could hardly miss?

"Shoot it, for God's sake!" William yelled. "Or we will never see daylight again."

The creature jumped forward. She closed her eyes and pulled the trigger, firing one barrel. The gun kicked, and blood splattered onto her dress as the creature fell across the ledge, then rolled over the side and into the pit.

William rammed shot and wad into his gun just in time, as two more creatures clambered onto the ledge. He stepped past her and held out the gun, and they backed away.

"They are blocking the path the way we came," he said. "We must try the other way."

They continued along the ledge as it curved around toward the entrance, walking backwards. If it went all the way, they could still reach the entrance.

Hope screamed as her foot slipped and she felt herself falling. William twisted around and grabbed her arm, his shotgun swinging free on its sling as he pulled her back up.

He held out the lantern. They had reached the end of the ledge, and, between them and the entrance, was a gap of several feet across the abyss.

A creature clambered up the pit on the far side of the gap. Its skin shone in the light from the lantern.

"Hold the light further out," Hope said. "We can see more, and perhaps it will scare the creature away."

William leaned past her and held the lantern at arm's length. The light illuminated a stream of water running into the cave from the tunnel, then across the ledge and down into the pit. It had been dry when they entered.

He glanced at the creatures approaching them on the ledge, then at the one near the entrance. He raised the shotgun and fired. The creature stumbled and fell to the ground, shrieking.

"We have to jump," he shouted, loud enough for Hope to hear over the ringing in her ears from the gunshots.

She nodded, and looked down into the gap. There was nothing to see but the bottomless black pit. Lightning flashed far below, and only darkness showed below that. If she fell, no-one would ever see her again.

They took a few steps back, to make room to run before the jump, but moving closer to the creatures that were approaching them. William put his hand on her shoulder.

"Go!"

She ran forward as fast as she could, and jumped. She flew across the darkness, the brief time she spent in the air stretching into what felt like minutes. Then her body slammed onto the slippery ledge, which knocked the breath from her lungs, and left her legs hanging back over the pit.

She lost her grip on the shotgun, and it began to slide back toward the pit. Her hands slipped on the wet rock as she tried to grab it, but her fingers caught the strap. As she slid back toward the pit, she dug her fingertips into the loose dirt on the surface of the ledge until she found some grip. Her arms ached as she pulled herself up.

The dying creature reached out for her. It lay on its back in the water flowing from the tunnel, and breathed laboriously as it tried to hold onto its life. For a second she felt pity for it, but this very creature may have killed Henry.

She didn't even want to touch it, but reached out a foot and pushed it toward the edge of the pit. It tried to hold on, but the force of the water and her push sent it sliding toward the edge. As it was about to go over it grabbed her leg.

She screamed and kicked at it. The creature continued to slide toward the edge, and its grasp pulled her from her feet. Her leg slid over with it, and its claws tried to pull itself up her calf. She kicked it in the face. It swung an arm, and she kicked it again, then again. Bone snapped, and its grip relaxed, then gave way.

The creature's shrieking echoed around the pit as it fell, then stopped as it thudded against the rock walls. Finally, a lightning flash lit the pit.

She heard another shot. William had shot one of the creatures with his revolver as it crept toward him, and wounded another. Kerberos lunged forward and bit the wounded creature. William raised the revolver and fired at it again.

"Jump, Father," Hope yelled.

He put the revolver in his pocket and turned toward her. Kerberos jumped and bit the creature on the neck, and it dropped to the ground. It squealed and shook as he tore at the creature's throat.

William ran toward her, and leaped across the gap. She stepped back, and he landed, slipped for a second, but found his grip. Hope held out her hand to help him away from the edge.

"Kerberos, come on," she yelled toward the dog.

He turned from the now dead creature, raced along the ledge, and jumped toward them. As he landed, she grabbed his collar, and pulled him to safety. Then took the nearest candle from the wall.

"We must escape before they overwhelm us," William said.

The water gushed from the tunnel, and the noise grew louder as it ran across the ledge and crashed down into the pit. The force of the flow had already knocked down some of the candles, and, while most of it was rushing directly out of the tunnel and down into the abyss, enough was flowing over the end of the ledge where they stood that the rock was now treacherously wet under their feet.

William pushed Hope toward the tunnel. As she stepped into the full flow of the water, it pushed her toward the pit, but she pressed herself against the wall to reduce the force it exerted on her, and grabbed any hand-hold on the rock to pull herself onward. The water soaked her legs, and the spray soaked her face and chest, as she struggled into the tunnel.

She could see the light of their candles ahead, and looked back to see Kerberos following her, and William behind him. The water was up to her knees, and they both struggled to push through it as she did. Kerberos raised his head to keep it above the water. He howled, and Hope glanced ahead. A rumbling noise came from further up the tunnel.

Suddenly, the candles ahead of them in the tunnel went out. The rumbling grew louder, and at the last moment she saw the large wave rushing toward them in the light from her father's lantern.

"Look out," she yelled, then grabbed for the tunnel wall, tried to find something that would support her. The rock was smooth, with only a few cracks.

The wave hit her, smashed into her legs and chest, knocked her candle from her hands, and put it out. It pulled her legs from under her, and she fell into the water, going completely under as she slid toward the pit.

CHAPTER NINETEEN

Hope tumbled through the roaring water, sliding back along the tunnel toward the pit. If only she had left with Pat the night before, she and her family would be alive and safe. She had done everything wrong in the last year, and would give anything to return to the girl she was then, and start all over.

Something grabbed her arm and pulled, and she gasped for breath as her face broke the surface. She opened her eyes, and saw William bracing himself against the flood as he held her. She tried to climb to her knees, and hung onto his arm as the water flowed past.

He pulled her arm, and reached out his free hand to grab her. He moved his foot as he leaned toward her, and it slipped out from beneath him. He slid back down the tunnel past her, and she slipped down again and followed. She slid around the tunnel in the water, scrabbling for grip on the wet rock, and lit only by the glow from William's lantern.

Until something stopped her. She grabbed for it, and pulled herself above the water. Kerberos had caught her dress in his teeth, and his paws slid on the rock as he struggled to hold her against the force of the flood. Her fingers reached for the wall, and found an outcropping on the rock. She pulled herself to her feet, but the flow was still pushing her back toward the pit.

Then the light went out.

"Father?" she yelled.

Even if he replied, she wouldn't hear him over the roaring flood, and couldn't see to search for him. He could have slid into the pit and vanished into the abyss before she could even try to save him. She pressed her back against the wall as the creatures screeched in the cave, and Kerberos barked at them.

Lightning flashed in the pit, and illuminated the tunnel. She was almost back at the ledge. Her hands and legs felt like ice, and, if she didn't return to the pit, she couldn't hold on much longer. She clung to and hand-hold on the walls as she crept down the tunnel. She would send a few of the creatures back to Hell before they caught her.

One of the creatures was hunched by the outcropping, watching her as she left the tunnel, and held back by the flood of water still flowing to the pit. Something moved on the ledge by one of the sculptures. William clung to it against the flow of water, with his legs dangling into the pit. He was struggling to pull himself up, and she reached out to help him.

"Thank God," he said as she helped him to temporary safety. "I grabbed it just as the water pushed me out of the tunnel." His jacket was caught on the sculpture, and he pulled it away. "Tore my damn jacket." He reached into the pockets, then glanced up at her with a frown. "And lost my damn guns."

Lighting flashed intermittently in the pit now, triggered by the falling water, and illuminated more creatures clustered around the ledge. The water that had threatened to kill them was now protecting them, as the creatures pressed themselves against the rock away from the lightning it triggered.

William looked into the tunnel, and the torrent of water still flowing out. "We must find another way out of this place."

More of the creatures crept around the ledge toward them. Hope pulled the shotgun from her shoulder, and held it up as she clicked the hammers back. Would it even fire, after the time she spent in the water?

Lightning flashed again. It illuminated her shotgun, and, beyond it, another tunnel entrance in the wall above them.

She pointed at the entrance.

"There," she said. If they could climb up the ridges on the nearby outcropping, then they could at least have a chance of escaping to the surface.

The nearest creature took a short step toward them along the ledge. Kerberos glared at it and growled, and it backed away again.

"Give me the gun," William said. "Then start climbing."

Hope grabbed one of the ridges on the outcropping to pull herself up, then climbed higher until she was almost level with the tunnel.

"What is up there?" William said.

She could see little in the dim glow of the walls, but a flash of lightning showed that the tunnel climbed steeply. Reaching it, though, would take a long jump.

"It goes up."

"Then that will do."

"I cannot see any more than that."

"I could hardly go somewhere worse. Anything that takes us toward daylight has to be the right way to go."

The creature moved toward them again. William pointed the shotgun at it, and it backed away. Kerberos barked and rushed forward, to grab one of the creature's legs in his teeth.

"Get to the tunnel," William said.

Hope looked back long enough to see Kerberos sparring with the wounded creature, and, in the next flash of lightning, more of them approaching him around the ledge.

"Kerberos," she yelled.

He turned and looked up at her.

The creature swung its claws toward him, but William raised the shotgun and fired the remaining barrel, hitting it in the face. It fell back into the pit. The others shrieked at its fate, the sound echoing around the walls until drowned out by a crack of thunder from below.

Kerberos clambered up the outcropping faster than Hope had. William grabbed the outcropping and climbed up behind him. The creatures crept forward along the ledge, covering their eyes briefly as the lightning illuminated them.

"Jump, for God's sake girl, before they reach us."

Dear God, if I ever return to the house, I will be a much better daughter than I have been before, Hope prayed. She took a deep breath, then leaped for the tunnel with all her strength.

Her chest and arms slammed down into the entrance, and she scrabbled briefly with her elbows and knees to pull herself into the upper tunnel. As soon as she found her footing, she heard a thud as William jumped behind her. She grabbed his arm and helped him up alongside.

A creature climbed up behind Kerberos and reached out its arms to try to grab him, but he jumped toward them. Hope crouched, caught him, and pulled him into the tunnel.

"Go," William said.

He pushed her up the tunnel and she struggled along it, well aware that the creatures would soon follow, once their hunger overwhelmed their fear of the lightning and rushing water. The shotgun was now empty, and they didn't have enough light or time to reload it, even if the powder in the bag was dry.

All they could do was put their hands on the walls in the darkness, and follow the steep tunnel as far as it would go, to wherever it would go. Hope's clothes were soaked through and the air was cold, and only the exertion of climbing stopped her shivering. Would she freeze to death before she reached the end of the tunnel? Screeching came from behind them. If she didn't die from the cold, at any moment, claws and teeth would slash into her from behind as the creatures caught up with them.

The glow from the rocks provided some light once her eyes adjusted to it, but she held out one hand ahead of her to warn her of any obstruction, and after a moment felt cold stone. She stopped, and William walked into her.

"What is it?" he said.

She felt around. Had the tunnel turned? Or come to an end? As she raised her hand, she felt an opening. "Something is blocking part of the tunnel."

She pulled herself up. As she put the weight on the obstacle, it moved beneath her, scraping against the tunnel walls. It must be a loose rock in the tunnel.

The screeching grew louder behind them.

"Hurry up," William said. Kerberos growled.

"Give Kerberos to me."

William picked him up, and Hope lifted him onto the rock, then slid down the far side and placed him on the ground. As soon as she did so, William climbed onto the rock, and it tapped against the tunnel walls as it rocked beneath him.

"Help me push this thing," William said as his feet touched the floor of the tunnel beside her. He put his weight against the rock, and it rattled and scraped against the floor.

Hope pushed alongside him, with what little strength she had left. The screeching echoed around the tunnels, and claws scraped against the walls just below them. Kerberos barked, and tried to squeeze past to attack them.

They pushed again. Hope leaned into the rock as far as she could, and almost fell as it began to slide away from them. Thuds of rock smacking against rock echoed around the tunnel as it accelerated down the slope, then a cacophony of loud screeches from the creatures as it approached them. She couldn't see them, but she could hear rapid thumps, then grunts and crunching noises, as the rock rolled into them.

"Hurry," William said.

Hope turned and continued up the tunnel as fast as she could go, with Kerberos now leading the way. They must have discouraged the creatures, but others would soon follow.

Then she saw a patch of light in the tunnel ahead, and the sight gave her fresh strength as she raced uphill toward it. Something lay on the ground ahead of them, silhouetted against the light. Scraps of rotten cloth, scattered over smashed bones. As she approached, she could see a rusted sword and a torn leather bag beside the bones.

William joined her, and examined the pile.

"It is too old to be Henry."

Kerberos sniffed around the bones. William handed Hope the shotgun and picked up the sword, then swung it in front of him as though he was back in his army days. He winced from the wound to his arm, and switched it to his left hand instead.

"At least we have something to fight them with," he said.

Hope lifted the bag by the strap. As she did so, the bottom fell out and spilled the contents onto the bone pile. Old candles, some of them gnawed, and the remains of some old bread, black with mould. Who was this who brought them there, and how long had they been in the tunnel?

As she bent down to examine the items, one of the creatures jumped from the dark tunnel behind them. It favoured one leg, as though it was one of those they hit with their rock.

William swung the sword, but the creature dodged out of the way. Kerberos barked and bit the creature's arm, which gave William the chance to stab the sword deep into its guts. Blood spurted on the wall as it fell to the ground.

Screeching grew louder in the tunnel behind them as more creatures approached. The one William had stabbed hissed at them, until Kerberos put it out of its misery by biting its throat. William pushed Hope onward. As they clambered toward the light, she stopped suddenly at the sound and sight of water ahead. The tunnel ended at a small cave, the entrance a few feet above a pool of water.

Where could they be? Her eyes scanned the pool, until she saw the rope dangling down ahead of them. The tunnel had led them to the bottom of the well. That explained why it had risen so steeply from the pit below.

William laughed and slapped her on the back. "We may live to see tomorrow after all."

Hope jumped into the water without thinking, intending to walk to the rope. She shrieked as her legs sank into the cold, clear water, and it rose up to her chest before her feet finally found the bottom. At least it wasn't as bottomless as the pool they had swum in.

William knelt and reached out a hand toward her.

"Look out," she shouted, as one of the creatures emerged from the tunnel behind him.

He turned in time to swing the sword. Old as it was, it cut clean through the creature's arm and into its side. It fell into the pool, and blood filled the water around its body.

William and Kerberos jumped into the water, and Hope led the way toward the rope. She heard more screeching and looked back. More creatures stood at the mouth of the tunnel, staring into the pool.

"Hurry," she said.

William glanced at the hissing mob of creatures, as they jumped into the water and pushed through it toward him.

The rope twisted and turned as the water flowed around it. Hope's knees grew stiff as her legs cooled from the exertion of struggling that far. They would give way at any moment, but only had to carry her the few yards from the pool to the house.

Kerberos swam up behind her. As she approached the rope in the far corner of the cave, the floor rose until he was just able to walk on the bottom, holding his head high. Hope grabbed for the rope as the water carried it past her, but her exhausted legs stumbled, and her arms missed it. She grabbed for it again as it swung back, and this time managed to catch it.

William stopped behind her, turned toward the creatures and swung the sword in their direction. One of them passed him and struggled through the water toward Hope. Kerberos turned and planted his teeth in its leg, which distracted it long enough for her to swing the shotgun barrels into the side of its head. It fell back into the water, and its arms and legs flailed as it tried to get up. Kerberos jumped onto the creature and bit at its neck. The creature tried to grab him, but its arms slumped down into the water before it could harm him. Kerberos climbed off the creature's dying body and returned to Hope.

William held two more creatures at bay with his sword. Beyond him, two more were climbing down from the tunnel into the water.

"Climb up, quickly," William said.

"How will Kerberos get out?"

One of the creatures tried to move toward William's right side, but Kerberos barked and jumped across toward it. It stepped back.

"We can pull him up in the bucket," William said. "If we live that long. Now, go."

Hope wrapped the rope around her body, lifted one of her feet to the muddy cave wall, and strained her arm muscles to pull herself up toward the opening. Kerberos looked up at her with eyes wide, as though he was sure he wouldn't see her again, and she hoped her father was right. Her arms ached, and her hands wanted to release the rope and let her fall back into the pool. She put as much weight as she could onto her feet, pushing herself up as her arms pulled.

Then her hand grasped the stones at the top of the well, and she pulled herself out, muddy and soaked to the skin. Rain poured down on her, and streams of water ran across the yard. The sky above was dark, night had fallen and the light they had seen was coming from the Moon through a gap in the storm clouds above her. It had only seemed so bright because their eyes had become accustomed to total darkness below. They had left the house in the morning, so how had they returned at night? What had happened to the hours in between?

She collapsed on the nearest piece of solid ground and breathed hard for a few seconds. Her body wanted to go to sleep, but she would never have woken again, succumbing to the cold, or the teeth and claws of the creatures following them.

She heard barking and screeching from the well and the sound brought her back from her stupor. She stood on unsteady feet, and leaned over the edge of the well.

"Father," she called into the well.

She could see Kerberos fighting one of the creatures at the bottom, and hear William yell. Kerberos jumped at the creature, which stepped back. He barked and lunged for it again, then vanished beyond the point she could see.

"Father," she called again, "I am on the surface."

He could still return to the rope and climb up. But the screeching and barking moved further away, as though they were pursuing the creatures back to the tunnel.

Something rustled in the bushes at the edge of the wood, and Hope looked up. One of the creatures stared back at her.

In the shock, she pulled the shotgun from her shoulder and turned toward it. The creature limped away.

"Get to the house," William shouted from below.

She pulled a cartridge from her bag and hurried to reload one barrel of the shotgun, so she would have some chance if she had to defend herself. Her hands shook from the cold, and she prayed that the powder would be dry enough to shoot.

Then she stumbled across the yard. She glanced back as the creature limped out of the bushes to watch her go. Why hadn't it attacked her? Was it was scared of the shotgun? Or, with the limp, didn't it feel that it could move fast enough to do so?

As she reached the lawn, she stopped and turned to check that nothing was following her. Something moved at the top of the well. Was her father climbing out?

Then the claws, and then the head, of one of the creatures rose from of the well.

She raised the shotgun, pulled back the hammers, and aimed at the creature. The barrels wobbled at the end of her exhausted arms, and the creature eyed her warily, then ran to attack. She pulled the trigger. The percussion cap fired, but the powder just fizzled.

She pulled back the hammers again, and fumbled in her bag for a fresh percussion cap. She tried to push it into place, but it slipped in her cold, wet fingers. She dropped it into the grass and fumbled in the bag for another. The creature swung its claws as it approached.

She tried to push the cap onto the shotgun, but she wouldn't be able to ready it in time, and it probably wouldn't fire if she did.

CHAPTER TWENTY

The creature jumped, and Hope raised the shotgun to use as a club. She screamed as its clawed hands reached out toward her. Then its head exploded, and she dodged sideways as the bloody remains flew past, landing at her side on the grass.

Pat stood in the study door with his musket, the light of a lantern glowing behind him.

"Hurry!" he shouted.

Another creature clambered from the well, and crouched as it crept toward her. She had to reach what safety the house offered before she allowed her body to collapse in exhaustion. The only alternative was death.

Pat dropped the musket, hobbled toward her, then raised his revolver and fired at the creature. He hit it in the shoulder, but it stood and ran on.

"Get inside," Pat said. Hope passed him as he fired a second shot, then a third. She didn't want to waste the time to look back and see the results.

She heard hissing and squealing from the well. Another creature ran around the side of the house, between them and the study door. If they didn't get past it, the creatures wouldn't just kill both of them, but could now enter the house through the open door and kill Eliza too. They had made a disastrous decision, and were now making it worse.

She stopped, and Pat caught up. He pointed his revolver at the creature by the house, and it backed up a little. He turned to the one approaching from the well, and it backed up too.

"Can you run to the door?"

Hope nodded. Even if it took the last of her energy, she would get to that door and through it.

Pat swung the revolver barrel from creature to creature as they approached. "Go!"

He fired twice at the creature in front of them. One bullet hit it in the shoulder, the other in the head. It dropped to the ground as Hope began to run.

As she passed the dead creature, she heard Pat fire the last bullet from the revolver. Then she was inside. Pat's musket lay on the ground blocking the door. With no cartridges to reload it, she picked it up and leaned it against the wall, then took hold of the door, ready to close it the instant Pat reached her.

He hurried across the lawn toward her. The creature was getting closer and closer to him.

It lifted an arm ready to swing at him.

"Look out," Hope shouted.

Pat glanced over his shoulder, and dodged out of the way as the creature tried to hit him. Then he was beside her. She tried to slam the door shut behind him, but the creature smashed into it before she could close it, and the impact threw her to the floor. The creature pushed past the door and into the study, then snarled at them.

Pat turned to the creature, which hissed at Hope as she tried to crawl away from the door. He hit it on the head with the butt of the revolver.

It turned and tried to bite him, but he swung the revolver toward it as he backed away. The croquet mallets leaned against a chair, and Hope crawled toward them, her limbs aching from the climbing and running.

The creature swung its claws toward Pat again, and hissed. He dodged a second time and pushed the door shut. It sat on its haunches for a second, looked at him, then lunged again. Pat dodged one clawed hand, but the other slashed his shoulder.

"Get back to Hell," Hope shouted at the creature.

It turned to her for a second, then snarled and turned back toward Pat.

She grabbed a mallet. Pat edged toward the door, avoiding the creature's wild swings. Hope held onto a chair with one hand to help herself to her feet as the creature passed between her and Pat. It snarled at him, and she hit it on the back. The mallet slid across its skin and down to the ground, with little effect, as her arms were as exhausted as her legs.

It turned and snarled at her. Pat reached for the musket where she had left it by the door. The creature turned to him. He wasn't going to die the way her father and brother had. Hope raised the mallet above her head, and swung it with all the strength she could still muster. The creature twisted around as she swung, but its skull crunched as the mallet slammed into the side of its head. It turned toward her and bared its teeth.

Pat grabbed the musket as the creature swung its claws at her. They swung past above her head as she collapsed to the ground, all strength gone. As it lunged again, he swung the barrel toward it. The skull crunched a second time under the blow, and the creature tumbled to the floor as Hope twisted out of the way.

Pat hit it again, the skull cracked and blood oozed out onto the carpet. Surely Uncle Howard would be upset to see the damage when he returned. Pat panted as he locked and barred the door, then he rolled the corpse over onto its back.

Hope looked up at him from the ground. "Is it dead?"

"So far as I can tell. But who knows with these things?"

He put the musket on the desk and reached out to help her up. With the immediate danger over, her body rebelled, and her legs collapsed.

He lifted her in his arms, carried her upstairs, and placed her on the bed. "Let me get you out of those wet clothes."

She sat up as well as she could, and he pulled off her boots, then between them they removed her bodice and the remains of her skirt. He continued removing clothes down to her chemise and dropped the rest into a cold, wet pile on the floor.

In a happier time, she might have appreciated the feel of his hands on her skin. Then he lit a fire for her, using some of the coal he had brought into the house.

"Turn away," Hope said.

He immediately turned toward her. She laughed.

"I need to change into my nightgown. You are not to watch."

Pat nodded and prodded the fire. Hope stripped the last of the clothes from her body, and slid the dry, clean nightgown over her head. She felt clean for the first time that day.

Pat prodded the fire with a poker. "Where is Mr Hodges?"

"I do not know. He and Kerberos were in the well, fighting the creatures to give me time to get away."

Pat nodded. "He may still get back here."

She shook her head. If only she could be as optimistic as he was. "The creatures got past him and out of the well. He would not have let them do that if he was alive. I am sure he is gone."

"Did you find any sign of Henry?"

"We found his clothes and marbles, but that was all. He has vanished from this world. I can only hope he has found peace in the next."

"Why were you gone so long? I thought those monsters must have caught you too."

"We cannot have been gone for more than an hour or two."

"You've been gone all day."

He sat beside her on the bed and put his arm around her. She leaned her head on his shoulder, glad of the warmth. "What do we do now? Everything has gone wrong."

"Like your father planned, we wait until morning and then we get away as fast as we can."

"What if those creatures come back? There are many more down in the tunnels and they have many tunnels through the ground below us."

"If we can't defend the house, we'll hide out in the cellar. In the morning, we just need enough time to get a mile or two down the track while the creatures are gone, we should be safe after that."

CHAPTER TWENTY-ONE

"After I saw you walk to the ravine," Pat said, "I went round the house searching for any way the dog could have got out. All I found was a broken window above the study. So, I got some planks up from the cellar to barricade the windows, and the rooms we're not using.

"When I was nailing some up on the window, I saw something moving outside, in the undergrowth. The rain was coming down like God having a beer piss, but two of those things were creeping toward the study. They saw me too, and then stopped and hissed at me. I shot one of the bastards, but the other ran toward the front door.

"So I reloaded my musket and went over to the dining room, where your mother was sitting. She kept asking if you were back, or if I'd seen your brother, while I hammered the planks over the windows.

"She said your uncle had been to see her, and I thought she'd gone nutty with grief, so I just nodded.

"Then she said he told her Henry isn't here anymore, and would be safe where he's gone. She said she didn't believe him, and he seemed upset when she told him you and your father had gone to look for Henry. He set off to try to stop you.

"So I just got on with boarding up the windows. When I picked up another plank, there was this horrid thud and crash from outside as one of the bastards butted its head against the glass, and smashed it. It hissed and shoved its head through the hole it made, trying to bite me.

"I hit it on the head with the plank. Broke the plank, but I broke its skull too, and knocked it down onto the broken glass in the frame so it cut through its neck. Your mother screamed like a banshee with all the blood spraying about, and that thing twisting and shrieking as it bled out.

"I pushed it out of the house and banged that plank up as fast I could, before I went to check the study. More of those things were crawling up the garden from the ravine.

"I took aim to shoot one with my musket. But then one of the creatures at the back of the pack raised its head and wailed louder than your mother. Was the first time I'd seen one do that, so I lowered the musket to see what they'd do. More of them started wailing, and more, until the ones closest to me turned and ran back toward the ravine, and the others joined them as they passed.

"I suddenly thought they must be going to look for you, so I shot one in the back as it ran away."

"If only you could have killed more," Hope said, "Father might still be with us."

"There were dozens of the sods. Not much chance of me making a dent in them unless they stood still and waited for me to shoot them."

He took a sip from a glass of Uncle Howard's beer before he continued.

"After that, I waited around, hoping you'd return while I worked through the beer and wine collection. By the time the sun went down, I was sure they must have got you, and just getting ready to fight them off another night. I didn't realize I was wrong until I saw you stumbling back to the house."

"The time away seemed like little more than an hour to me."

"More like ten or twelve to me."

"Perhaps it is related to the problems with Uncle Howard's clocks. Time does not seem to work here the way it does in London."

He smirked. "From what I gather, nothing works here the way it does in your London."

Hope leaned forward and held onto him. He put down his beer, pushed her down onto the bed and leaned over her, slid his hand under her nightgown and explored her body. She let him entertain himself that way for a moment, then pushed the hand away.

"Not until we are married." She had made a promise to God, and perhaps that he would protect them if she kept her side.

"We could be dead before morning."

"Then I will meet Father in Heaven, and will tell him I have not been a worse daughter to him than I was before. Besides, I am tired, and your back is in no condition for love games."

Pat nodded. "I'll check none of the creatures are outside."

Then he left.

Hope lay back on the bed. Her limbs felt like lead weights, and she wanted nothing more than a good sleep. But every time she closed her eyes, she saw her father slipping through the water toward the pit, or fighting those demonic creatures in the well. Perhaps she could calm down enough to sleep if she wrote them in her journal?

As she wrote, she heard rain pattering on the window. She stood and looked out. Not rain, but the garden was covered with a thin layer of snow, even though this should be summer. Perhaps her mother was right when she said the creatures have broken time. And she could understand why Howard would run away. Living in *Tartarus* for even for a few days would make anyone a fitting inmate for Bedlam.

The shrieking of the creatures woke her. The fire had burned down to embers in the fireplace. How many hours had she been asleep? For a moment there was silence, then the shrieks began again.

She slid from the bed and looked into the hallway outside the bedroom. The door across the hallway was open and a candle burned inside. Pat moved in the dim light.

"What is happening?" she said.

He turned toward her, and winced as he moved his leg. "I've been patrolling the house since you fell asleep. They've been sneaking through the garden in ones and twos. I don't think they're going to attack us tonight, but they don't seem to want us getting much sleep."

The creatures shrieked again. Hope walked across the room to the window, and Pat put his hand on her shoulder as they looked out. A creature sat on the lip of the well.

Pat lifted the latch and opened the window. Freezing air blew Hope's nightgown around her, and she stepped back out of the wind. Pat raised the musket, aimed at the creature, and fired. Its head flicked back as blood splashed over the snow. Then it fell backward into the well.

Pat crouched and began to reload the musket. The creatures shrieked louder, then stopped.

"How long have you lived near here?" Hope said.

"All my life. Near enough."

"Have you ever seen weather like this before? Snow in mid-summer?"

He shook his head. "This is the strangest weather I've ever seen. And the sun goes down early like we're in the middle of winter. I won't be upset to see the back of this place."

Hope looked out of the open window. Snow had built up on the windowsill, and more was falling gently from the sky. A few trails of clawed footprints crossed the garden, but she could see no more sign of the creatures than that. Something moved in the corner of her eye, and she glanced toward the wood. A bush moved, and a creature rushed between two trees. They were still out there. If they built up in a mass on one side of the house, they could all attack at once. Two people could do little, if two dozen creatures broke through the windows at once.

Pat finished reloading, and closed the window. He took her hand and led her back to her bedroom. She lay on the bed.

"Do you think we will survive the night?" she said.

"I'll stay here and watch over you, miss. You need sleep, and if I hear anything more I can investigate."

"I fear that, if I sleep, those creatures will take me before I awake. Earlier I thought perhaps they had given up, but they just seem to be biding their time, waiting for something."

"If a few creeping around in the dark is the best they can do, miss, I figure we've got a good chance. You and Mr Hodges must have discouraged them."

He sat on the bed, and winced as he did so. The bandages were slick with blood, and more was seeping through them.

"How is your back?"

"It hurts, but I'll manage."

"Let me see."

Hope sat up. Pat turned round, and she began to unwrap the old bandages from his body. The cuts glowed dull green in the candlelight, and the skin around them was turning grey as though infected, forming ridges around the cuts.

"How is it?" Pat said.

What could she say? Clearly this wasn't how he should have healed, and the grey, scaly skin looked like the creatures who had been attacking them. Hope reached out a finger and touched the ridge beside one of the cuts. The skin was hard and rough.

"It may be diseased."

As she ran her finger along the cut, the glow intensified.

"I will clean it again. We must find a doctor when we reach the village, or this could become a mortal sickness."

Pat fetched fresh bandages and alcohol, and Hope cleaned the wounds as best she could, then bandaged them again. Had the creatures spread some disease to him? Her father, too, had been suffering from his wound, and perhaps this infection would allow the creatures to kill them without a fight. That was another good reason to leave the house in the morning, if the creatures let them live that long.

Hope imagined her father, staring down at them from Heaven, alone together on her bed, Pat half-dressed, her in her nightgown. Were he not already dead, the sight would make his heart give out.

But they might be dead any moment.

"Do you think Father would really begrudge us one night together?"

Pat looked into Hope's eyes. "I don't reckon what he thinks matters much right now."

"We may not have much time left before we join him. I would like to live as much of the rest of my life as I can before it is over."

He stroked her hair. She leaned forward and kissed his lips. He held her face to his as his tongue explored her mouth. She could taste the beer he had drunk during the day.

She reached down and lifted the hem of her nightgown. He helped her pull it over her head, and drop it to the floor. Then he kicked off his shoes, and unbuckled his belt. She helped him pull off his trousers and underpants. The small things she had seen down there when he was swimming were much larger that night.

He pressed her down onto the bed and kissed her again, then his lips worked their way down her neck to her breasts. His hand pushed her legs apart, and he climbed in between them.

CHAPTER TWENTY-TWO

After he was sated from love-making, Pat climbed off her and rolled on his side. In a moment he was snoring, all thought of patrolling the house or watching for the creatures long gone.

Hope pulled her nightgown back on, and lay beside him, his sweat cooling on her aching body. The novels made the first time a girl gave herself to her lover sound like it would be the most wonderful time of her life, but she just felt more bruised and broken than before.

What would become of them? Perhaps she should be afraid she was carrying his baby, but it seemed a minor fear compared to the others. In the unlikely event that they survived, she would be glad to deal with an unexpected child there and then.

Her mind raced as it retraced everything that had happened that day, but her body was exhausted, and couldn't stay awake for long. She should have been mourning Henry and William, but, without proof of their death, she could still hope they would return. Perhaps her father chose the right name for her after all.

She woke to find Pat gone, and the bed collapsed beneath them. Not only had all the furniture collapsed, but the floor too, and dropped her onto the remains of the bed in Mrs Phillips' room below. How could she have slept through that? Then she saw the floor was covered by a thick layer of dust and fragments of furniture and floorboards, the wood charred. The windows were just frames and rusty bars, and more dust shimmered in the light shining through them. The house hadn't collapsed while she slept, unless she had been asleep for many years.

This must be another dream.

She clambered from of the pile of wood and rubble that had been their beds. The door must have collapsed long ago, and she stepped toward the empty frame, moving her feet from one clear spot to another between the debris. She heard a continual crackling around her, but couldn't see where the noise came from.

The hallway floor was covered with dust and broken, charred wood, and black stone showed through large holes in the hall wallpaper. She strolled out of the arch where the front door once stood, and looked up at the house from the outside. The roof had collapsed, the windows and doors decayed, and grey bricks from the walls lay scattered around. The remains of the house were composed of a single block of the black stone, as though the builders had found it on the cliffs and built the brick walls around it. The stone was the only part of the house that had survived the years with no sign of decay, as though it had never been part of the time it exists in.

She sat on the steps. The house stood between rows of black stone machinery that reminded her of those they had seen in the tunnels. They were as tall as their house in London, and made the steam engines at the Exhibition look like toys.

Lightning, the source of the crackling she had heard earlier, flashed between the machines and the upper floors of the house, as though it was just another part of the strange machinery. Perhaps that is what it had been all along?

Was she dreaming, or had she really travelled to another time? Did the distinction make a difference when the dreams seemed so real? She walked down the steps, wishing she was wearing more than her nightgown as it fluttered around her in the wind blowing between the rows of machines. The house was in shadow and the sun was setting behind the machines, so it provided little heat to warm her.

The creatures wandered between the machines just as she had seen in the tunnels, some attending to the machinery near ground level, while others worked high up on scaffolds. She walked into the deeper shadows near the machines, hoping that none of the creatures had seen her, and that they would be so blinded by the bright light of the lightning that they wouldn't be able to see.

Could she really be transported into some unknown future overnight? She had left the house for less than two hours the previous day and returned eight hours later, and, overnight, they had gone from summer to winter. The way things had changed around them before, who was to say what could or couldn't happen there?

She crept through the shadows toward the next machine, trying to stay out of sight of the creatures as she watched them at their work. They moved from place to place, reaching their hands inside the machines, or removing parts from one section of the machine to carry them to another. Lightning flickered around them, but they seemed unperturbed by it, neither the flashes, nor crackling, nor booming interrupting them. Perhaps, now they lived on the surface of the Earth, they had lost the fear of light that had served her and her father well before.

She heard a skittering noise and crouched in the shadows, and wished her nightgown wasn't so glaringly white. She looked up and saw a metal spider climbing down the side of the nearest machine, staring at her with a dozen shining black eyes. She stood and backed toward the house. More of the spiders climbed over the nearby machines to look at her.

She heard skittering behind, turned her head and saw one of the metal spiders clinging to the front of the house, watching her. She was surrounded, with little hope of escape. The spider's legs tapped as it climbed down the house.

She ran toward the door, and any safety the house might provide. The spider swung its front legs toward her, but she dodged past and into the doorway, relieved for a moment that she had avoided it, but determined to go as far into the house as she could, so the spiders couldn't follow her in. Then she looked up. With the roof and floors gone, they could simply crawl down the interior walls.

She passed what had once been the dining room and study, and looked for a hiding place. The doorway at the top of the cellar stairs was open, with only a few pieces of metal among the debris indicating where the door once stood. She reached it a few seconds later, and looked inside. The stairs above it had collapsed, and the staircase down to the cellar was blocked by broken floorboards and furniture, which ended any hope she had of finding a hiding place down below where she might evade the creatures.

She heard movement behind her, and turned. One of the creatures stepped into the hallway, holding a long spear of dark stone in its hands. This was the first time she had seen them use a tool of any kind, and, for a second, she was more surprised by this new behaviour than scared of what it might do. It looked around the hallway, then stepped toward her and thrust the spear point toward her chest.

She stopped and awaited her fate. Alone in her dream in a world run by these creatures, what else could she do? She pinched herself, and tried to open her eyes back in her real bed before it could harm her, but nothing worked. Her heart beat faster. Could she have slept through centuries after all, then awoken alone far in the future?

"I mean no harm," she said. The creature stopped for a second, then pushed the spear forward.

She screamed as lightning flashed from the spear point to her chest. Her body shook uncontrollably as the lightning sparked across it, her heart beating at a crazed pace in her chest, and her legs collapsed beneath her.

The creature jumped forward, and followed it into the house, hissing and shrieking. She tried to struggle, but her limbs wouldn't move. The creatures dragged her across the room to the door, and her nightgown caught and tore on the broken boards as they did so. She tried to scream as they dragged her naked to the steps, but her voice would no longer obey her either.

The creatures carried her along the alleyway between the rows of machines until they almost reached the cliff top, then turned to the south and carried her toward the ravine. More of them were working on the machines on that route, and they turned to look as the others carried her past. She felt strength returning to her arms and legs, and tried to pull herself from the creatures' grip. For a second, she succeeded in pulling a foot from the claws of the one who held it, but two more jumped down from the nearby machine and helped them to restrain her. The creature with the spear held it up and prodded her. She stopped struggling, before he used the lightning again, and settled for studying the creatures as they worked.

They seemed far more organized than those she had met in her own time, working together rather than acting like hungry, crazed animals. Was that how they had grown powerful enough to leave the tunnels, or did something else control them, which had told them to move above ground? Either way, it didn't bode well for her. If the creatures in her own time had been that organized and worked together, they wouldn't have survived for long. Even if the creatures didn't have the power to create lightning at will.

They carried her to the ravine, where the true extent of the horrific future became apparent. Much of the cliff had fallen away, and a tall waterfall replaced land where they had once walked at the end of the ravine. On the far side of the ravine, a fence reached twenty feet into the air, the bars seemingly made of lightning buzzing between pillars of the same black stone as the house. A narrow bridge of black stone stretched over the gap, and they carried her across it toward the fence.

Behind the fence was a sea of people, packed together. Men, women, children, all naked as the day they were born, just like animals on a farm. If the creatures planned to eat them, she would do everything in her power to kill a few more of them first.

Dozens of creatures walked along the fence and peered in, pointing their spears at anyone who approached the bars of lightning. Those carrying her walked toward it, and, as they approached the fence, the sparks between the nearby pillars stopped. The creatures stepped through the gap, dropped her on the ground, where the remaining plants had been trodden into the dirt by thousands of footprints, then backed up until they were outside. It sparked again.

Now, she was trapped with all the others, and her only means of escape was to wake up. Her arms and legs tingled, but otherwise seemed to work. She pushed herself off the ground and sat up on the dirt, trying to cover her nakedness with her hands as she studied the people around her. They were dirty and looked poorly fed. The enclosure smelled of sweat, urine and shit, just like a human farm.

A woman crouched nearby, holding a baby to her chest.

"Have you got any food? I need food, we haven't eaten in days."

The baby, was thin, lay on her arm with its eyes closed, and barely breathed. Its head flopped back and forth as the woman moved.

"I am as naked as you are," Hope said. If she had carried any food into her dream, the creatures would have taken it from her long ago.

As the woman looked away, Hope grabbed her arm. "What happened? What are these things?"

"They came out of a storm last week," the woman said. "They went round the village, and rounded up everyone who couldn't get away, then brought us all here. They've been bringing more in ever since."

"How did they build this place?"

"There was nothing here before the storm, just the old ruin. It was like the city just appeared from nowhere overnight."

Hope heard a rapid thumping noise. A flock of dark birds flew through the sky toward the enclosure, and, as she watched them, the sound grew louder. Streaks of fire flew from the birds, leaving long trails of smoke behind them. Some of the better fed men and women around her cheered at the sight, then lightning flashed from the machines to the ends of the fire streaks, which exploded.

The birds turned away, close enough that she could see that they too appeared to be some kind of machines. More lightning flashed toward them, and the flying machines caught fire and fell into the sea. The cheering ended as fast as it had begun.

Hope turned back to the woman, but she had vanished into the crowds. With her body shivering and nothing better to do, she sat on the ground waiting for something to happen, her knees pulled to her chest and her arms wrapped around them as some protection against the cold wind. The sun sank toward the sea, and they would soon be shivering through the night. Would she survive until morning without freezing, if she didn't wake up back in her bed?

Feet stomped on the dirt and sparse grass as the others moved around the enclosure, and legs thumped into her back. She yelped as a heavy foot crunched down on hers, the man whose foot it was glanced silently at her, then disappeared into the mass of prisoners. She stood, so no more would step on her.

Walking around the perimeter of the enclosure would warm her up, and she might find some means of escape. Male eyes glanced at her as she stood there naked, and she tried to cover her body with her hands as she squeezed through the crowd around her.

"Nice ass," a tall man said as she pushed past him. She glanced back at his face. Hair billowed around his face in uncontrolled curls, a rough beard covered his cheeks and chin, and dirt was smeared across the skin.

His hand grabbed for her arm, but she twisted away and squeezed through the first gap she found between the people ahead. Despite their fate, some men never seemed to stop thinking of fornication. Or perhaps their fate was what caused them to think of it, as with Pat and herself.

She heard gun shots, and pushed herself up on tip-toes to look between the nearest gap in the crowd. Lights flashed among the distant trees. At first the shots were rapid, and blood erupted from two of the creatures who then fell to the ground. Lightning flashed toward the trees, and the shots slowed, then stopped. Whoever shot at them had retreated or died.

As she walked on, she heard girls screaming. As the crowd moved around her, she glimpsed piles of naked bodies, male and female, writhing on the dirt. The creatures guarding the fence ignored them, and continued patrolling past.

Two men grabbed a young girl up ahead, and she screamed as they pulled her toward the others.

"Get away from her," a bearded man yelled, and pushed through the crowd toward them. More men and a woman pressed toward them and tried to pull her away from the two who held her.

The newcomers wrenched her from the clutches of the men, and the woman comforted her while the other men punched and kicked those who had tried to take her.

Hope backed away. She couldn't help, and, if she stayed there, they might grab her, too. Her back pressed against a warm body behind her, and she turned her head to look for a way past. A fat man stared down at her. He put his arm around her waist, and pulled her to him.

"Where's your family?" he said.

She tried to pull away, but he held her tighter.

"I do not know."

He smiled at her. "Then no-one's going to come looking for you, are they?" He nodded at the men who had tried to take the girl, who now lay bleeding in the dirt while other men and women kicked them. "That's where they went wrong."

He turned her around, pushed her to the ground and climbed on top of her. She pounded her hands on his sides and shouted for help, but the crowd just backed away to make space for him as he kissed her neck and fumbled with her body. She pulled her arm back and tried to punch him, but he deflected her blow and held the arm down in the dirt. She yelled louder, twisted her hips and tried to knee him in the groin.

Then part of the fence stopped sparking again. A dozen creatures stepped through the gap, crouched low with spears held out before them. Some of the men tried to grab the spears, but the creatures thrust the points forward and lightning flashed from spear to men. They fell back.

A creature prodded the fat man with a spear, and he looked up. They pressed the spear against his chest and pushed him away from Hope. He slid from her and sat back on his heels. Had they come into the compound to rescue her?

She should have guessed they had darker goals in mind.

The creatures circled a group of two dozen people, men and women alike, half of the creatures using their spears to prod them out through the hole in the fence, while the other half kept the rest of the crowd at bay. One prodded Hope's side with his spear and she climbed to her feet, then he pushed her toward the gap.

A moment later they were outside, and the fence began to spark again. Another creature came close, dragging something dark and shiny behind him. He wrapped a thin chain around their ankles and wrists, which twisted on its own accord and locked itself into place. It felt warm and light on her skin. She twisted her arms, trying to pull them free, but the chain held them tight.

"Get off," the girl ahead of her said as they wrapped the chain around her. Fair hair was tied up at the side of her head, like the girl Pat had mentioned from his dream.

"Who are you?" Hope said.

The girl turned toward Hope. Her body was scratched, and blood was smeared on her cheek.

"Emma," she said. "What do you want?"

"My..." she wondered how to describe Pat and settled for "friend... saw you in a dream."

Her eyebrows furrowed, and she backed away. Perhaps that wasn't the best way to put it.

"He said he saw these creatures attack you in the tunnels," Hope said.

"They killed my family. Leave me alone."

Emma cried and struggled against the chains, then the creatures pushed them apart as they chained the others.

The creatures chained the fat man several places further up the line from Hope. At least she was safe from him, but would the fate the creatures had planned be any better?

A spear point prodded her back. The creatures strode along the line, prodding the men and women until they began to move. The chain grew tight as those in front began to walk, and Hope followed. The fat man looked back at her and scowled.

"It's all your fault. If it wasn't for you I'd still be back in the camp."

What could he fear more than being trapped behind that fence with all those starving people, now acting little better than animals? Hope glanced at the man behind her, who was older than her father, his hair completely white. "Where are they taking us?"

"Buggered if I know. Every day, they take some people away, and they never come back. Who cares? I'd rather be dead than spend the rest of my days starving among other people's shit back there."

The fat man shook his hands against the chains. "You've killed me, you stupid cow. I'm gonna kill you before they do."

Blaming her for his misfortune when he had tried to force himself on her seemed laughable, and more reason to believe this was just another dream. But this was the first dream she had dreamed as herself, and showed no sign of ending. After Henry's disappearance, and dreaming of it beforehand, how could she tell whether anything she saw was real or imaginary?

The creatures led them further inland, away from the house. Most of the woods had gone, replaced by rows of their machines, and only the lightning flashes illuminated the moors around them.

They turned, and followed another narrow alley between the machines. The glow from the black stone was bright enough to light their way, and the lightning bolts flashed so bright against the night sky that, at times, she had to cover her eyes. At the end of the alley they turned again, and for a short walk to a large open space. The machines stood in a circle around it which must have been miles across, as she could barely see those on the far side. Only the lightning flashes made them visible in the dark night.

Inside the circle, was the town or city she had seen in the ice-covered land. Was that before or after this dream? The city didn't exist in her time, so either that dream was the future of this city, or, if her mother was to be believed, the machines were saving the city from the ice by somehow transporting it into the future.

The creatures pushed them along the alley. Two led the way, two followed behind, and the others lumbered beside them. The older men looked down at the ground, seemingly accepting whatever fate the creatures had in store for them. Most of the women looked around them, and had little choice but to follow anyway, and any who fell behind were pulled along by the chains.

The fat man shook his wrists, and pulled them against the chains, but the thin loops of metal held. A younger man stopped just behind him. The chains pulled tight, and those at the front of the group turned to see what was happening, while those at the back stopped to avoid walking into him.

"I'm not going any further, you bastards," he said.

Three creatures approached him, spears held ready to strike. He glanced at the others in the group. Then he yelled, and jumped toward the nearest creature. His hands clamped around the shaft of its spear, and he tugged on it, trying to break the creature's grip. Hope took a step forward. If they all tried to help, perhaps they could beat the creatures. But the others huddled together under the glaring gaze of the remaining creatures on guard, and the chains pulled tight around her wrist.

The man pulled the spear from the creature's grip and swung it around to block the second creature's attack. But that exposed his back to the third.

"Look out," Hope yelled as the third creature swung its spear. He twisted toward her, and his eyes bulged in surprise. Then the blood-covered point of the creature's spear emerged from the man's stomach.

As the creature pulled out his spear, the man slumped to the ground and blood oozed from his wounds.

The creatures swung their spears, hitting the fat man on the back. Another creature prodded Hope with his spear. The men at the front moved on, and the others followed, dragging the mortally wounded man by the chains. After a few moments he no longer moved.

Would they jump on the body, and tear it apart with their teeth and claws? For now, at least, they seemed to consider their work as escorts and guards more important than their taste for flesh. Could this be another example of their new organization in the future?

The fat man glanced back at her now and again as they trudged onward, his face frozen in a perpetual scowl. Sweat ran down his forehead, and across his bare chest. He seemed too tired or scared to make more threats.

They trudged on toward the circular building, and the road between the houses widened as they approached it. Lighting flashed between the machines and the building, and between the building and its surroundings, illuminating the area like day.

When would she wake up? Part of her wanted to wake there and then, while the rest wanted to stay and see where the dream would take her. But what if it wasn't a dream?

The creatures stopped, and the group came to a halt between them, pulled around by the chains that held them together. Hope looked up into the face of the fat man only a foot away, and he swung his arms toward her. She tried to step back, but the man behind blocked her way. The fat man grabbed her arm. As she tried to pull out of his grasp, the creatures raised their spears and fired lightning at him. He fell to the ground, and lay there twitching as one of the creatures walked around the group, splitting them into men and women on two separate chains.

"What are they doing?" Emma said.

"I have no idea. I never saw them this organized before."

"How do you know so much?"

Before Hope could answer, the creatures prodded her again, pushing the women and girls toward the tall circular building, and the men toward one of the low buildings. Two young men tried to grab the creatures, but backed away as the spears fired lightning at them. One struggled on regardless, getting his hands around the neck of the nearest creature, before his brave attack ended with a spear point through his neck.

As the creatures led the men away, the fat man took one last look at Hope. "I'll see you in Hell."

The building they approached looked like a painting Hope had seen of the Coliseum in Rome, but built from the same black stone as the house. Lightning illuminated it, and more gargoyles like those on the house stared down at them from the walls. But these weren't stone, and twisted and glared down at them as they passed.

They walked to a hole in the tall black walls, where a tunnel led to the interior. A long scream came from behind them, and Hope looked over her shoulder. It must have come from the building where they had taken the men, and muffled shouting followed from that direction. Then a creature hit her ass with his spear, to encourage her onward.

As they reached the end of the tunnel, the interior opened into an elliptical arena. At the far end, a crowd of creatures were hunched on the ground as though praying. But to what? A tall throne of black stone sat in front of them, lightning arcing to it from the frame to the building. In the throne sat another creature much larger than the others, with wide eyes, large wings and horns. For all her father's talk about Hell, she had never imagined that she might see the Devil for real. But he seemed to fit the description, like the creature from the wall paintings and sculptures in the tunnels. Was this their leader, who had now organized them in a way that they couldn't do themselves in the past?

As she stared at him, he looked up from the crowd, and for a moment his eyes met hers, cold, dark and unblinking like a wild animal. She looked away, hoping that she would soon wake. The others whimpered and muttered to themselves as the creatures pulled them inexorably toward the demon on the throne.

One of the creatures in the crowd turned toward them, and began to limp in their direction, like the one who had watched her in the garden that day. As the others led them on toward the throne, the limping creature passed by the other women in the line before Hope, then stopped. His head turned from side to side as he looked at her, and he could smell rotten meat on his breath.

Then he grunted in a low, guttural voice, sounding like an animal, yet speaking in English.

She woke from the dream with his words echoing in her ears. If she didn't know better, she would say it was Uncle Howard's voice, but probably just an illusion she created in the dream. Pat's arm lay across her body. As she lay there, he reached up and ran his fingers through her hair.

She rolled onto her back and found herself staring into the face of one of the creatures. It leaned over and kissed her.

She woke, mouth open wide, heart thumping, and her lungs ready to scream. Light glowed around the edges of the curtains, and she had survived to see the new day. She turned her head and looked at the other side of the bed. Pat lay on his side, still human.

He rolled over and stretched. "You getting up, miss?"

"I do not think you need to call me miss any more. Call me Hope."

"Doesn't seem right, miss."

"What we did was not right. Father will be cursing me from Heaven right now."

Pat stroked her shoulder. "Felt right to me."

She lay back. He smiled and slid across the bed. She could see his intentions in his eyes. Only then did she realize that she was no longer wearing her nightgown. Where did that go? Could she really have left it in the future?

His hand stroked her stomach, then slid up her chest.

"Doesn't this feel right?" he said.

"Father was always sure what was right and what was wrong. I no longer have any idea."

"Don't you love me, miss?"

She looked at his sunburned face and the strong fingers that squeezed her breast. She imagined herself old and grey with him in a cottage by the sea, a gaggle of children around them. Well, she supposed she must do.

She nodded.

"Then what we did was right."

He rolled onto his front and slid a leg between hers. Then he stared into her face, smiled, and climbed on top of her. The bed creaked as his weight pressed the mattress down.

His muscular arms pressed against the pillow beside her head and he entered her less painfully than the night before. She looked into his eyes as he slid in and out of her body.

"We should get up," she said. "We have to leave before the creatures find us."

He sucked on her neck. "I won't be long, miss."

With the bed creaking beneath them, she didn't hear the approaching footsteps until the door opened. Eliza looked in, her face taking on an unaccustomed look of horror.

"Whore!" she shouted. "Your father has not been gone a day, and you are whoring in his house."

Pat raised his head. "Oh bugger."

"Mother," Hope shouted, but she fled the room.

Hope struggled beneath Pat's weight as she tried to get him off her.

"What is it?" he said.

"Get off me."

"Let me finish. I only need a few seconds."

"No, get off."

She slapped his bare backside. He pulled out of her and climbed off, and she tried to sit up. He put his hand on her shoulder and held her back.

"Chasing after her won't help."

"What have I done? Will she now stone me to death for whoring in my father's house?"

"You're no whore, miss."

"I feel like one."

"Besides, this is your uncle's house."

She could have laughed, but not when her own mother thought of her that way. She pulled a sheet from the bed and wrapped it around herself.

"I should never have let you do that."

"Didn't seem like you let me, miss. More like you wanted it and I helped you."

He was right. As much as he wanted her that night, she had wanted him more. In the strain and fear of death it had seemed like a good idea, but now, in the light of day, she could perhaps see herself surviving and returning home, and couldn't imagine what any husband would make of her. She was ruined forever, all for the sake of a moment of lust. She finally understood why her father had tried to keep her away from him.

"I must see my mother," she said.

He pulled himself toward her. "Let's finish what we started first. We may never get another chance."

"I think we started quite enough. Start packing, we should leave as soon as we can. I will try to convince Mother to come with us."

CHAPTER TWENTY-FOUR

Hope dressed properly, picked up the shotgun from where it leaned against a chair, then crept downstairs to the hall. She shivered in the cold air, and pulled Mrs Phillips' scarf tight around her neck. It had come in useful after all.

Eliza sat in the dark beside the dining table, staring at the window. There was nothing to see, as Pat had boarded it up the previous day.

"I had a bad dream," she said.

Hope sat across from her. "I have had bad dreams too. They seem to be a part of this place."

"I dreamed that everyone but Howard had left me. I was alone in the gardens looking for Henry. At least you have not gone, even if your father has."

"I would not leave you, mother."

"Howard says we must leave immediately, but I will not go until Henry returns to us." She stared into Hope's eyes. "When will you search for him again?"

What could Hope say? Their only chance was to leave as soon as they could. Even one more night might be more than they could survive. "I will speak with Pat."

Eliza shivered. "I wish he would fetch more coal, the house is so cold. And there is no water, he must fetch more from the well."

"Mother, we cannot drink from the well. Those creatures are down there."

She had to find Pat to discuss how they could leave the house and return to the village. And how they would convince her mother to go, or force her to go with them, if they couldn't convince her to leave willingly.

She descended the spiral staircase into the cellar. She could hear scraping and rattling. A light glowed in the distance, as Pat moved some of the stores around.

She shivered again as she remembered what was at the far end. She wouldn't go far into the darkness, but she had to see Pat. He looked up at her, and nodded as she approached him.

"Give me your hand," he said.

She held it out, and he took it in his, then pulled her fingers toward him.

He reached into a pocket and pulled out something that shone in the light of the lantern. He raised it toward her. An old, worn gold ring with small gems encrusted in the sides.

"Where did you get that?" she said.

"Down here among your uncle's things. I don't think he'll mind us making good use of it." He gazed into her eyes. "Will you marry me?"

Her parents wouldn't have given their consent. But since she didn't know whether they would live to see another day, she couldn't worry about what might happen months or years in the future.

She leaned forward and kissed him. "Of course I will."

"You don't think your father will mind?"

"You have already taken my maidenhood, he could hardly complain about you taking my hand."

"I fear these creatures will not let us live long enough to find a priest."

If they did, it would be a miracle. She nodded. At least they could die together rather than apart.

He placed the ring on her finger, and her heart fluttered. She had always imagined her wedding would be in a church, but that morning the cellar seemed perfect.

She raised her hand and studied the ring, which already felt as though it had been on her finger forever. "This morning I dreamed that I met Uncle Howard."

"Where was he? Back in London?"

She shook her head. "Here, I think. In the future. He was one of the creatures."

Pat smiled. "No wonder we couldn't find him, if he's been dressing up as one of the creatures and hiding in the future."

"He spoke to me."

"What did he say?"

"Go home."

Pat kissed her again. "Then he gives good advice. We'll leave as soon as you're ready."

"Can Mother really walk twenty miles through the snow?"

"She'll have to, if you want to get away from this place. If we stay, and we're lucky enough to survive another night, the snow could be worse tomorrow."

A scream came from above. They ran for the stairs.

Eliza stood by the front doors, screaming. Had one of the creatures broken into the house? But Eliza pulled the door open, with a keyring in her hand.

"Mother, stop!" Hope shouted. "You cannot go out there."

"I will not leave without my son. I must find him."

Then, before they could reach her, she threw the door open and rushed outside.

"What's she doing?" Pat said.

"She has gone mad. She thinks that Henry is still out there."

Pat pulled the revolver from his belt as they approached the door. They rushed outside, where Eliza was lifting her legs high to push her way through the drifts near the house.

"Henry," she shouted. "Henry!"

More snow fell from dark clouds above them. Lightning flashed in the clouds and arced between the towers on the roof of the house.

"Mother! Stop!" Hope shouted, but Eliza continued onward.

She struggled onward, trudging through snow above their knees. Pat was taller, but his leg slowed him down.

"Henry!" Eliza yelled as she strode through the shallower snow drifts along the edge of the ravine.

With all the noise she was making, if they didn't get her back to the house in the next few minutes, the creatures wouldn't let them get back. The clouds above blocked the sun that might have scared them away, and indentations in the snow showed where they had walked overnight and left footprints to be filled in by the storm.

"How did she get out?" Hope said.

"I left the keys on the chest of drawers outside the lounge. I never imagined she'd do something like this."

As they reached Eliza, Hope grabbed her arm. "Mother, stop this."

Pat stared down into the ravine, his revolver at the ready. "Mrs Hodges, we must return to the house. It's not safe out here with those things around."

Eliza struggled as she tried to pull her arm away from Hope. "I will find Henry, even if you have abandoned him to those things."

She lashed out and pushed Hope away, and Hope fell on her back in the snow. Pat tried to grab Eliza, but she scrambled down the slope into the ravine. He grabbed Hope's hand, and helped her up instead. "Are you all right?"

"I am fine. We must stop Mother."

She was at the bottom of the ravine, by the stream.

"Henry," she shouted, louder than ever.

The shouts would attract every creature in earshot. More tracks in the snow climbed in and out of the ravine and along the bottom near the stream, where the water struggled past patches of ice.

She should turn and run back toward the house before the creatures reached them, but she couldn't abandon her mother. As Pat clambered down the slope, the bushes shook further down the ravine.

"Pat, watch out," she yelled.

He continued toward Eliza.

"Mrs Hodges. We must leave here now."

"Henry, come here," Eliza shouted.

A creature ran from the bushes toward them. Pat raised the revolver and fired three times. The second shot hit it in the chest and the third in the head, and red blood sprayed over the snow as it fell.

Eliza glared at him, and covered her ears with her hands. "Stop that noise!"

Hope slid down the slope toward them. Her legs dug into the snow, which oozed into her boots and froze her feet.

"Mother, we have to leave. Howard said that Henry is not here. We will return to search for him in better weather and bring other men to help."

Bushes moved further down the ravine. Another creature was coming for them. She raised her shotgun toward it, then saw the familiar texture of her father's checked jacket. Could he have survived after all?

"Father?"

"Henry, where are you?" Eliza shouted.

"Pat, get her away from here."

A half-human face appeared in the bushes, the other half grey and scaly like the creatures. Then it pushed through and emerged into the light, the body and legs creature-like, the arms covered by William's jacket.

It lumbered toward Eliza.

"William?" she said.

"Mother, get away," Hope yelled.

Pat raised his revolver and aimed at the creature. Hope opened her mouth to tell him to stop. Had the creatures turned her father into this misshapen thing? But her mother stepped toward it, and it continued stumbling through the snow toward her.

Pat fired twice, and his second shot hit the creature's shoulder. Then it moved behind Eliza, and she blocked his view.

Pat stomped sideways through the snow, trying to move around her. Hope stepped forward and slid the shotgun from her shoulder, ready to use it as a club if she couldn't use it as a gun. The creature grabbed Eliza's shoulders. She screamed as it lunged forward and bit into her neck, and blood sprayed out around its mouth. Pat fired, but his shot went wide.

The creature raised its blood-covered face toward Pat, and dropped Eliza's body. It turned again, and for an instant its eyes met Hope's, with an expression of pain on a familiar face.

"Father!"

Its gaze roved between her face and Pat's. Then it jumped toward him. Pat's gun was empty, and he raised it to use as a club. Before it could reach him, Hope aimed the shotgun, fired and blew a bloody hole in its chest. It fell to the ground.

She didn't want to look at the thing. That couldn't have been her father. Or, if it was, anything human that remained would have welcomed its demise. She knelt by her mother's body, but Eliza's breathing slowed, and she went silent.

Pat grabbed her shoulders. "Come on. We have to go."

She grabbed Eliza's shoulders and pulled. The body barely moved an inch. "I do not want those things eating her."

Pat pulled her away. He motioned toward the bushes, where two more sets of eyes peered out at them. "Come on."

They struggled toward the house as fast as they could, with the creatures following. So far, only two had found them, and a third watching them from the woods. The creatures still seemed apprehensive of the overcast daylight.

They ran back into the house and slammed the doors closed, locking and barring them. The creatures thudded into the door, and their claws scraped down the wood. More thuds came from the planks Pat had nailed over the windows in the dining room. She stepped along the hallway, peering into the shadows. Could any have entered the house while they were gone? She stepped toward the study door, but Pat grabbed her shoulder. Glass was breaking behind it.

"Two of us can't fight them off," Pat said. "We need a place we can defend."

Hope nodded. They would have to wait for the creatures to tire of attacking, then make their way to the village as fast as they could.

The creatures bashed and scraped on the study door. They must have found their way in through the study windows, and were now trying to enter the house proper.

"We can hold out in the cellar until they give up," Pat said.

"But then what?"

The dining room door was open. One of the creatures crawled through, glaring at them.

Hope swung her shotgun, but Pat pushed past her toward the creature. If she fired, she would hit him too.

It rushed for Pat, dodged his attack and knocked him to the floor. Then it bit into his shoulder.

She stepped forward, raised the shotgun, and put it to the creature's head, then pulled the trigger. Blood and gore spurted from its head, and it collapsed on top of Pat.

She crouched and tried to pull the creature off him. He pushed himself up on his good arm, and helped her move it away.

He pulled the keyring from his pocket and handed it to her. "Get to the cellar. There could be more in here."

She helped him to his feet, and they stumbled toward the door. It was still open. But, if one creature had come in, more could be waiting for them down there.

Behind them, rapid thuds crashed against the study door. The top hinge broke free and it twisted out across the hallway. One of the creatures forced its way past. Hope pointed the shotgun toward it and pulled the trigger. Hammers clicked down on empty chambers.

The stairs creaked. Another creature was creeping down the steps toward them, where it could get between them and the cellar door.

"Go," Pat said, and tried to pull himself away from her.

"I will not lose you too," she told him. But he pushed her away, and turned to face the creature behind them.

"You saw what happened to your father. I'll be one of the bastards soon. Get away while you still can."

The creature screeched at Pat. He pushed himself to his full height and screamed back at it. The creature on the stairs jumped down toward Hope, and she swung the shotgun. Ribs cracked as she hit it in the side, and it backed away.

The other creature swung its claws at Pat, catching his arm. It swung again, but he blocked the blow and punched it hard in the stomach. As it reeled back, Hope raised the shotgun and swung the stock into its face, breaking its nose. It staggered back.

She grabbed Pat's arm, to pull him toward the cellar. He twisted it from her grip. "I will not leave my husband," she said, "no matter what he is going to become."

The creature behind them lunged toward her. Pat stepped around to block the attack.

Its teeth bit into his neck, and he fell to the floor. Hope screamed, and it turned toward her. Then it turned back, and began to chew on Pat's body.

She swung the shotgun and hit it hard on the back of the head, but the other creature climbed over Pat's body and glared at her, its lips pulled back to expose its teeth.

Kerberos jumped from the stairs and sank his teeth into the creature's leg. The creature screeched, then swung an arm, and knocked Kerberos across the corridor. How had he escaped from the well, or found his way into the house? He must have found a tunnel to the surface, and entered through the front door while it was open.

She ran for the cellar, and Kerberos hobbled behind her. She slammed the door and locked it as the creature ran toward them. Kerberos hobbled down the stairs as she barred it, then she followed. The creature bashed against the door and the bars rattled, but Howard's defences kept it shut. If they did get in, she would barricade into the final room at the end of the cellar. Beyond that there was nowhere left to hide.

Deep within the cellar, glass smashed, and claws scrabbled at the windows as the creatures outside tried to break in. As Hope reached the bottom of the steps, she found Kerberos waiting, the one and only reassurance in a cellar which looked dark and uninviting. She had no lantern, and the only light came from the tiny windows high above.

She stepped into the darkness. She could find a lantern in the stores, reload the guns for some protection against the creatures until she could try to escape. She would send a few more of them to Hell as revenge for Pat and her parents.

As she stepped forward, she heard a crunch in the darkness. She stopped to listen. More crunching echoed around the cellar. Kerberos crept toward the noise. Hope grabbed his collar and held him back. He whimpered at her restraint.

The noise stopped. She waited for a few seconds. Had she imagined it? She was hardly in a state for rational thought. But it began again. She crept toward the pillar the noise came from. Please let it be a rat. She held the shotgun ready to hit anything hiding there.

The pillar was where they had left Mrs Phillips' body, and her heart sank. The blankets were torn and bloody. One of the creatures was hunched over her remains, chewing.

It turned and looked up at her. Then rose from its meal and crept toward her.

She jumped back, as Kerberos crept forward. He was already wounded, and she didn't want to see him killed by this creature for no reason. She pulled him back by the collar, while he growled and tried to pull away from her.

The creature stopped, and turned its head from side to side as it studied her. Then it stepped closer. Outside the house, the other creatures screeched louder, thumping on the walls and barred windows.

It jumped toward her. She swung the shotgun at it, but the creature grabbed it, pulled the gun from her hands and threw it across the cellar.

She dodged away, but it spun around. It jumped up at her, and she screamed as it knocked her onto her back, and its claws tore her dress. Its teeth snapped at her face, but she twisted her head out of the way, then pushed one hand under its jaw and tried to press its head back.

Kerberos nipped at the creature's ankles, barely damaging it but distracting it for a second. Its teeth lunged for Hope's neck, but caught her dress instead, tearing cloth rather than flesh.

She looked for a weapon. Kerberos bit again, and this time the creature squealed and twisted toward him. Hope pushed with all her might. The creature flew back and smashed into one of the wine racks. Bottles fell from above as one side of the rack collapsed. Glass smashed on the ground all around them.

Kerberos snapped at its heels. It kicked at him, then pushed itself back up. Hope rolled away across the pool of wine, trying to avoid the broken glass, and grimaced as a piece cut her shoulder. She grabbed the neck of a broken bottle as the creature lunged toward her with jaws open wide. Kerberos bit into its heel, distracting it enough for her to dodge the attack. She thrust the sharp spike of glass on the bottle's neck forward, and it slammed into the creature's eye.

The creatures outside screeched, and the one inside pulled its head back. Blood spurted from the wound, and it squealed with pain. Hope dodged the flailing arms as Kerberos lowered his head and bit the creature's legs. She reached out, grabbed the glass and twisted it, even though the edge cut into her hand.

The creature pushed itself up, pulled its head away from her, and swung wildly as it tried to slash or kick Kerberos.

She grabbed another piece of glass, and stabbed the creature in the chest and stomach, as Kerberos' jaws snapped at anything they could reach. The creature's screeching filled the cellar as Kerberos' teeth crunched down on its balls.

With a long squeal, it fell to the ground, and lay whining as its life drained away. Kerberos sat back, muzzle coated with the creature's blood. Hope panted from the exertion, and examined the gashes on her hands where the glass had cut them.

She clambered past the creature's body and picked up one of the chunks of black rock. It turned its head for a moment and looked at her with its good eye. She raised the rock and brought it down hard on the creature's head, which cracked as she hit it. The breathing stopped.

She pulled a chunk of glass from her arm. Kerberos rubbed around her legs, and the creatures watched them through the windows, scrabbling and jabbering as they retreated deeper into the cellar, toward the stores.

The creatures shrieked outside the house. She reloaded the shotgun and began to shoot at them through the windows. They shrieked much louder as buckshot and glass tore into their bodies. A moment later they were gone.

After that, everything was quiet. The cold stone floor sucked the heat from her body, and she found some blankets in the trunks to keep herself warm. Snow fell, and piled up outside the windows. She stacked pieces of wood that Howard had left down there, and built herself a small fire. The flames barely warmed her, but, if she built it any larger she could set the house on fire. Burning to death wouldn't be much better than being torn apart by the creatures.

She should have taken Pat's offer to elope and live with him when he first made it, which seemed half a lifetime ago. If she had, they would have been living happily together, and Henry and her parents would have left the house to search for her.

Her own choice had damned them all, yet she only made that choice to please her parents. Perhaps her mother was right about Uncle Howard. God must hate their family to have chosen to destroy it in such a horrible manner. Hope was the last, for Howard never married and William had no brothers or sisters. If the girl in the village was really carrying Howard's baby, she hoped it would have more luck than she had.

She ventured to the locked room, and picked up Howard's notebook. They would need all the help they could get against the strange creatures and their machines. Howard must have been looking for a way to defeat the creatures himself, and the book could contain something indicating a weakness, or a safer route into the caves.

She lit a circle of candles around her makeshift bed, then sat beside Kerberos with gun and cartridges at the ready. They wouldn't give their lives easily, and, if they could find a way to reach the village, would return to destroy the creatures forever.

AUTHOR'S NOTES

This novel began around 2003. I was working on indie movies in London and reading Lovecraft and Hodgson again, and I'm still fond of the old tropes of remote houses and horrible monsters, so I decided I should write a screenplay.

As it became more complex, the budget soon rose beyond the level anyone I knew could raise, and the script sat on my hard drive for years until I decided to rewrite it as a novel. It's a rather different story, but the basic plot and characters remain.

I originally published it as 'Tartarus', but I liked Uncle Howard so much that I really want to write a series based on his adventures, and that version of the novel wouldn't fit with the style of those books. So this is the new, improved, and final version of the story that began so many years ago.

ACKNOWLEDGEMENTS

Many thanks to Lizz Syme and Zahra Brown, for their beta-reader feedback and proof-reading.

ABOUT THE AUTHOR

Edward M. Grant is a physicist and software developer turned SF and horror writer. He lives in the frozen wastes of Canada, but was born in England, where he wrote for a science and technology magazine and worked on numerous indie movies in and around London. He has travelled the world, been a VIP at several space shuttle launches, survived earthquakes and a tsunami, climbed Mt Fuji, assisted the search for the MH370 airliner, and visits nuclear explosion sites as a hobby.

Find him online at www.edwardmgrant.com.

ALSO BY EDWARD M. GRANT

PETRINA

Brother Thomas hoped he had an easy job, collecting an experience recording for the Abbot. But when he stepped out of the Monastery into the World, his blood-soaked past returned to haunt him.

Peter Kaine thought he'd found an easy job. But the unwritten rule of bounty hunting is that your second client is never as easy as the first.

The crew of the Big Momma thought they'd found an easy job, carrying cargo to the backwater asteroid of Petrina. But life is never easy around the kind of passengers willing to pay for a cabin on their ship.

SMILING IS CONTAGIOUS

Tired of healing wounded soldiers on the borders of the British Empire, Silas Cane returns to the heartlands of Victorian England as a rural doctor. The quiet Oxfordshire village is a welcome break from the chaos of war, until a smiling madman dies of a disease never seen before.

After watching so many men die, Cane will do whatever it takes to keep the villagers alive.

If they don't kill him first.

A 14,000 word science fiction horror novelette.

ROBO-ZOMBIE

Darren's Robo-Rat project would have saved countless lives, allowing rescuers to go places no human could survive. If only the zombie apocalypse hadn't interrupted its funding.

Now he's trapped on a hotel roof in Saskatoon with his boss, while the girl he loves fights zombies far below. But Rob the zombie, a case of electronics, and a cordless drill may offer a chance to rescue her after all...

A 7,500 word science fiction horror short story. With remotely-controlled zombies.